Rescue Me

The Men of Honor Series

LARA VAN HULZEN

MOSAIC PRESS

Rescue Me, Men of Honor, Book 3
First Edition
© 2015 Lara Van Hulzen, All rights reserved.

www.laramvanhulzen.com

This is a work of fiction. The characters and events portrayed in this book are fictitious and otherwise imaginary and are not intended to refer to specific places or living persons. Any similarity to real persons, living or dead, is coincidental and not intended by the author. The author has represented and warranted full ownership and/or legal right to publish all the materials contained in this book.

No part of this book may be reproduced, or stored in a retrieval system, or transmitted in any form or by any means, electronic, mechanical, photocopying, recording, or otherwise, without express written permission of the publisher.

ISBN 978-1516990009

FOR NATE & COLE

May you be Men of Honor. Always.

1

TORIE BOLTED UP in bed.

Thunk!

Yep. She'd heard a noise in the kitchen. Moving with the stealth that years of being a cop had taught her, she grabbed her gun from the nightstand drawer and silently headed down the stairs.

Barefoot, she made her way to the kitchen, careful to not make a sound. Staying close to the wall, she listened as she moved.

A drawer opened and closed. Someone was definitely moving around the kitchen. But opening drawers? What were they looking for? What would a robber want from the kitchen? And how the heck had someone found her way out in the mountains?

Her blood ran cold and she gripped her gun tighter. She knew exactly who could find her. It was the reason she'd agreed to stay at Dane and Aimee's cabin while they were on their honeymoon. It was secluded and safe. Or at least she'd thought so until now.

Was that humming? There was a man in the kitchen humming. Okaaay.

She peeked around the doorway into the kitchen. His back was to her, his broad shoulders blocking most of the window above the sink where he stood.

"Hands up!" She braced herself in the doorway, gun pointed, every fiber of her being on alert.

At first the man didn't move. He didn't raise his hands either. Interesting.

He took a deep breath, let it out, then turned to face her. Crossing his arms over his broad chest and leaning back against the counter, he said, "Good morning, Torie."

Keith.

She dropped her arms, her gun now dangling by her side. "Oh. It's you."

He smirked. "Not exactly a greeting that's good for the ego, but okay." He pushed away from the counter and took his coat off, draping it over the back of one of the kitchen chairs.

The man was massive. And gorgeous. And someone Torie couldn't stop thinking about since they'd met a few months ago. He looked rustic and manly and outdoorsy standing there. She couldn't help but notice how the button-down shirt he wore, tucked neatly into Wranglers of course, showcased his muscular forearms. For heaven's sake, the man was one big mountain of muscle. She suppressed a sigh.

Keith turned back to the counter and moved two cups of coffee along with a plate full of pastries to the kitchen table.

"I brought you some breakfast."

She groaned. A fact she'd missed because A) she was freaked someone was in the kitchen and B) Keith had been standing in front of it and hello, who could look at anything but him? The man practically demanded to be ogled. At six-foot-five with sandy blond hair cropped military style, blue eyes that shimmered, and a physique that said, "I was a Greek god in a past life," Dane's brother was pure eye candy.

Torie managed a quiet, "Thank you," before pulling out a chair and plopping down into it.

She laid her gun on the table and pointed to the other chair. "Please sit."

"You sure? You won't shoot me or anything, will you?" His eyes twinkled and dimples peeked out as he smiled at her.

"Um, no. Sorry about that." She took an almond croissant and a napkin and dove in. Goodness, these things were sinful. And worth every calorie.

Keith took the seat across from her. He grabbed an enormous bear claw the size of his hand. They chewed in quiet for a moment, the ticking of the wall clock the only sound.

Torie loved it here. She was a country girl at heart. She'd

lived in San Diego for a few years working as a police officer, but her true nature was wide-open spaces, not the city.

"You want to tell me why you felt the need to pull a gun?"

She wasn't going there with him, that was for sure. Answering a question with a question always worked. "You want to tell me why you didn't even flinch?"

He shrugged, took a bite of pastry and chewed. Guess he wasn't in a hurry to answer her questions either. He took a swig of coffee and leaned back in his chair.

"I heard you coming down the stairs. By the way you were moving I figured you thought I was unfriendly."

He'd heard her? What was he, part rabbit?

"I also knew you wouldn't shoot me. You're a good cop. You would never pull the trigger unless you had to."

"How do you know I'm a good cop?"

"Instinct. And Dane said so." There was that smile again that made her bones go gooey.

Dane was Keith's brother and a cop. Well, used to be. He was also now married to Aimee, Torie's best friend and former roommate. Dane and Aimee met in San Diego but decided to live up north, near Lake Tahoe, once they were married. Dane quit the police force to help Keith run the family cattle ranching business. Aimee offered their cabin to Torie while they were gone over Christmas so…here she was. With Keith. In the cabin kitchen. Munching pastries with her gun sitting between them. Her life was never boring, that was for darn sure. Boring would actually be nice for a change.

She'd hoped for boring when she agreed to stay up north through the holidays. But with Keith around, that was highly unlikely.

"So is breakfast the only reason for this lovely visit?"

He raised an eyebrow.

"Not to sound ungrateful. This croissant is downright decadent." She took another bite.

"My parents wanted me to check in on you. See if you needed anything."

"That's nice of them."

Colt and Ellie Scott owned the 4S Ranch and the land the cabin sat on. Keith had his own place on the other side of the property. Torie had never seen it, but she was curious, for sure. Keith was an enigma. One she wouldn't mind figuring out.

"You're our guest. My parents' southern hospitality will worm its way in whether you like it or not." He smiled then bit into the bear claw again.

She smiled back and took a sip of coffee. Although she was looking forward to time alone, hanging out with the Scotts sounded nice. When Torie accepted her friends' offer of the cabin, she knew it was the perfect place for her to hide out, decide what to do next. Only when she got to the cabin did she realize she'd worked every Christmas she could remember to avoid the sense of loneliness that overwhelmed at times. Being with the Scotts would help her avoid it. And she was safe with them. That was a nice bonus.

Keith finished chewing and took a sip of coffee. "My

folks are protective as well. They know you're important to Aimee, so that means you're part of the family. We take care of family."

A lump formed in her throat and "That's nice," was all she could come up with in response. The concept of a loving, protective family was foreign to her on many levels.

"What about your family? You don't want to be with them for Christmas?"

His question dug into her thoughts.

She shook her head. "No family."

"You don't have family?"

Torie wasn't surprised he couldn't wrap his head around that, especially with the loving family he had. The Scotts were kindness and acceptance personified. Loyal to a tee as well. She knew that much about them. They'd stepped up and helped protect Aimee not long ago when she was in trouble, with hardly any questions asked. And simply because she was important to Dane.

She shrugged but didn't answer.

He crossed his arms and eyed her from across the table. Her heart skipped a beat and not because of the caffeine in her coffee. More from the way his steel blue eyes bore into hers, attempting to accept her cryptic answer.

Not sure if he would continue his inquiry about her family or not, she stood and started cleaning up the plates from the table. She took them to the sink and rinsed them before placing them in the dishwasher. Keith still didn't say anything. Normally that kind of quiet with people made her nervous, but with him it didn't. Huh. She shrugged and added her coffee mug to the dishwasher as well.

A movement outside the window caught her eye.

"There's a dog out there!"

Keith stood and joined her at the sink, the warmth of his presence not lost on her. He smelled of pine and leather and fresh air. She breathed in deep, trying to quietly soak him in for one blessed moment.

"You're absolutely right. There is a dog out there!"

His teasing tone made her laugh. She swatted him with a dishtowel that had been lying on the counter.

"That's Bones. She my best girl."

His best girl? Torie had never in her life been more jealous of a dog. "Bones, huh? Not exactly super creative there, Big Boy."

Keith looked down at her with a smirk. "You're brave enough to try a nickname with me, are ya?"

At six feet tall, having someone actually look down at Torie was unusual. But he didn't intimidate her. She actually appreciated his size. For once a man didn't make her feel like a giant. "Sure. Why not? Although maybe Captain America is more appropriate since you've got the whole smoldering, kick-butt soldier thing going on."

Did she just say smoldering? Out loud? She turned and hung the dishtowel on the rack by the stove. Anything to avoid his eyes.

He chuckled.

Changing the subject was a good idea. "So, why do you call her Bones?"

He shrugged. "I like the TV show."

She may have imagined it, but she could've sworn he blushed. To say it was cute didn't justify how much more attractive it made the man. "Ah, so you have a thing for smart women like the lead character on the show. I can respect that."

He looked at her, his eyes the color of a summer sky and said, "No. She's not my type."

Torie swallowed hard, afraid to ask what kind of woman *was* his type. She did, however, find her voice enough to say, "She's a beautiful dog. What breed is she?"

He looked back out the window. "She's an Australian Cattle Dog."

"I've never seen that breed before."

"They're perfect for ranching. Bones is one of the best dogs I've ever had."

Torie watched as Bones scratched her ear with her back paw then sat tall, ears perked towards the woods. The left side of her face was black with brown spots and speckled with white. The right side of her face was more white with black speckles. She was a patchwork of neutral colors and regal in stature.

Torie could hear in Keith's voice that Bones meant more to him than a work partner on the ranch. She was his buddy. Torie'd had that. Once. But the outcome was so painful she tried to forget about it. Yet another glaring difference in the way she and Keith grew up. Their worlds couldn't be more opposite.

"I better get going."

His deep voice brought her out of her thoughts.

"Oh. Sure. Of course. I'm sorry to have kept you. I'm sure you have lots of ranch things to do today."

"Ranch things?"

"Well, yeah. You know…" She waved towards the window.

He laughed and put his coat on before opening the back door.

"Thanks for breakfast."

He nodded. "Sure thing. I wrote down my cell number and my parents' numbers over there." He pointed to the corner counter in the kitchen. "I also left you a walkie-talkie. Sometimes that's easier than the phones when we're out on the property."

A warm feeling moved through Torie's middle. She was being watched over. Cared for. It had been way too long since she'd felt that. She missed it more than she realized.

"Thanks. I appreciate that."

He took his Stetson off a hook on the kitchen wall, put it on, and tipped it to her in a nod. "Have a good day."

He ducked out the door and down to Bones, who wagged her tail then stepped in beside him. He opened the door of his truck and she climbed on in, her sweet doggy face smiling. He started the truck and with a wave, drove away.

Torie closed the door and eyed the paper and walkie-talkie. This might be a better holiday than she thought.

* * *

Keith's truck bounced along the road between Dane's cabin and his. Wanting their boys nearby, his parents had made sure they could build cabins where they wanted, far enough away for privacy from the main house, but still on Scott land.

He listened as Sam Hunt sang about leaving the night on and tapped the steering wheel. Aware that his mother was playing matchmaker once again, he hadn't fought her on paying Torie a visit to welcome her and make sure she was okay and all set at the cabin. He hadn't expected the hitch in his pulse when he turned to see her pointing a gun at him. However, he was more distracted by her pajama pants with Santa hats on them and the Keith Urban concert T-shirt she wore. Not to mention her beautiful long blonde hair mussed from sleep that was sexy as hell.

Torie strolled into his life a few months before when Aimee needed protection from a thug who was chasing her. As Aimee's roommate and a cop, Torie helped apprehend the guy and put him behind bars.

She was staying at the cabin for the holidays. No family, and for some reason she was jumpy. Interesting. She hadn't caught him off guard when she pulled her gun on him. He was a highly trained United States Marine. But he was curious as to why she felt the need to be so paranoid out here on his family's land. Didn't she know she'd be safe? Something haunted her and he wanted to know what.

She'd been a large part of Keith's thoughts since he'd laid eyes on her. She'd pulled up in her old beat-up truck and his heart had pulled towards her in a way he didn't think it ever would again. He'd been breaking in a new horse that day and almost fell off when she got out of her truck, all six feet of her, and made her way towards the corral. She'd really gotten his attention, going toe to toe with him about the plan to catch the thug chasing Aimee. Few people dared. Certainly not a female.

But his gut told him there was more to this woman than met the eye. Tough and beautiful exterior. Lonely on the inside. He saw it in her eyes. Definitely when he'd asked her about family. His curiosity was piqued for sure, and he had every intention of getting to know more about Miss Torie Walker.

He rubbed behind Bones's ears and chuckled.

"This is going to be an interesting holiday season indeed, sweet girl."

Bones looked at him and grinned.

2

WELL, NOW WHAT?

For the first time since arriving at the 4S Ranch, Torie questioned her decision to stay through the holidays.

She had taken a shower and dressed in her comfiest jeans and a dark blue turtleneck sweater. She stood in the middle of the living room and looked around. Dane and Aimee had done a nice job with the place.

The living room had a deep brown sofa and love seat with an ottoman in front. An alpaca rug lay before the fireplace. Knotty pine walls and ceiling made for a pure cabin feel and windows lined the front and side of the house, looking out to the wraparound porch and lush fields beyond. Huge pine trees outlined the property, creating a wall of woodsy protection.

It was rustic and homey. Inviting. Made you want to kick

off your shoes and cozy up by the fire for a while. But as appealing as that sounded, Torie was too wound up. Did she ever stop working long enough to just sit and stare? No. She didn't. And she knew why. Letting her mind wander meant too much of a chance for old ghosts to creep in and poke around.

Leaving a few days before to enjoy their honeymoon in Colorado, Dane and Aimee had left the keys to Dane's truck in case she needed it. But she preferred her old pickup. It was the first thing she'd bought after getting a job on the police force, the first thing that had ever been truly hers, and she loved it. Every last faded red inch of it.

She grabbed her coat and keys. Maybe strolling through town would cure her anxiousness.

Tahoe City bustled with activity. Christmas garlands and big red bows adorned the old-fashioned lampposts that lined the street. Snow had fallen the night before but the streets were clear now, only the sidewalks were patched with white.

Torie parked her truck and watched people go by. Couples carried shopping bags. Two women chatted and sipped coffee as they walked. A little girl being pushed in a stroller munched a giant cookie shaped like Santa, her reindeer hat sprouting antlers out the top. Torie could almost see Christmas cheer floating in the air. Loneliness washed over her. The interior of her truck became a cocoon separating her from those outside full of hope and joy.

Maybe this wasn't such a good idea. She was debating

driving right back to the cabin and holing up there when she spotted a sign that said Cozy Corner Books. It had been a while since she'd lingered in a bookstore. The idea had promise. Climbing out of her truck, she headed down the street.

Snow crunched under her boots as she walked. She loved the feel of the cool air mixed with the warmth of the sun on her face. Memories of her time spent in Wyoming came to mind. The good years. Years she'd spent with Gram. Not all her ghosts were unfriendly.

A bell tinkled above the bookstore door as she entered. The smell of leather and paper filled the air as well as the scent of coffee. Torie breathed in deep. Pure heaven. She'd gotten a love of reading from her Gram, but hadn't had much time for it lately. Maybe she could catch up on a few of her series while she was here. And, that would keep memories from creeping in too often. Bonus.

She wandered over to the shelves that held historical fiction. Yet another thing she inherited from her Gram—a love of history. As she ran her fingers over the books, she spied a new one from one of her favorite authors and pulled it out, turning it over to read the back cover.

"I didn't peg you for being the reader type."

Keith's deep whisper in her ear jolted her out of her trance and caused her to jump. The book dropped to the ground with a thud. His hands reached out to steady her as he chuckled. "Sorry. Didn't mean to scare you."

She faced him, one hand over her racing heart, the other over her mouth to stifle a scream. Goodness! What was her problem? She wasn't jumpy, or a screamer. She berated herself for letting her guard down, even momentarily. It could cost her if she wasn't careful.

"I guess I'm better at sneaking up on you than you are at sneaking up on me." His eyes twinkled at the reference to her attempt at catching him in the kitchen that morning.

Standing in the aisle of the bookstore, he still held her shoulders, his body taking up most of the space between the shelves. His blue eyes looked down at her from under a light tan Stetson. Her heart continued to race, not from fear anymore but rather Keith's presence, which wrapped around her like a security blanket.

When she didn't respond he said, "Hey, are you okay? I'm just teasing. I really am sorry I scared you." He let go of her arms and bent down so they were eye to eye.

She nodded and removed her hand from her mouth. "Yes. Yes. I'm sorry." She let out a breath. "You did scare me, but I'm okay."

He bent down and picked up the book she'd dropped and handed it to her. "Here you go." He looked at the cover. "Historical fiction? Hmmm, I'd see you more as a True Crime kind of girl."

She smiled, her heart rate slowed, returning to normal. "One would think so, right? But no, I get enough of that at work."

He nodded and shoved his hands in his jean pockets. "Makes sense now that you say it. People always think I'd want a military book to escape. Not sure how they figure that, but they mean well."

Sadness flashed in his eyes for a moment then was gone. Torie could only imagine what he'd seen and done as a soldier. The idea of Keith in harm's way made her stomach turn. She shivered at the thought of the danger he faced in his job.

"Are you cold? They have fresh coffee here. It's good too." He winked at her.

She shook her head. "Um, no thanks. I'm good. I'm jumpy as it is, apparently. No more caffeine for me."

He smiled.

"What kind of book are you looking for if you don't read military?"

"Well, I know it's sort of stereotypical, but I like old westerns. Louis L'Amour, that kind of thing." He leaned towards her and whispered, "And sometimes I like Science Fiction. But let's keep that between us."

"Your secret is safe with me," Torie whispered back. She couldn't help but soak in the irony of this enormous mountain of a man whispering like a little boy about his secret love of Science Fiction. Keith was living proof that you can't always judge a book by its cover. His cover was enticing, and the inside story was something she definitely wanted to read more about.

He stood straight again. "I'm here today though looking

for a book for my mom for Christmas."

"Oh, that's nice. What does she like to read?"

He frowned. "Romance novels."

Torie laughed out loud. The woman working behind the counter gave them a look but then continued with her task.

"Hey now. I didn't say *I* was reading them."

"I know." Torie couldn't stop laughing. "I'm just picturing you standing in front of the romance novel section of a store and getting some…stares." But mainly because he belonged on a cover. She didn't add that last part, of course, but her brain sure went there. Keith without a shirt on *had* to be romance novel worthy. Her cheeks warmed at the thought.

"I don't know much about that genre, but Aimee reads them all the time. I could try and help you pick some for your mom."

The relief that washed over his features was priceless. This fierce warrior in front of her wound up tighter than a drum over picking a book had her laughing again.

"What? Why are you laughing now?"

"Nothing. I think it's nice, actually, that you would go to such lengths of discomfort to get your mom a Christmas gift."

He smiled and looked at his boots. "Yeah, well…"

Ah, a rough exterior with a soft, gooey center. Keith was becoming more and more appealing by the minute.

"You wanna wait here while I go look in the romance section?"

"Nah. I'll brave it with ya." He winked and put an arm

around her to lead her down the rows. His warmth was not lost on her. Nor the unique scent of him that was setting up residence in her memory.

Fifteen minutes later, they'd chosen three books Torie was sure his mom would like, and Keith made his way to the counter to pay. The woman bagged the items and gave him his change. He nodded to the woman and turned to Torie.

"Thanks for your help."

"Sure. Anytime."

"You headed back to the ranch?"

"Not yet. I think I'll sit and read a bit. Check out what magazines they have."

He nodded. "Sounds good. See you later then."

"See ya."

He stepped towards the door but then turned to her again. "Oh. I almost forgot. Mom wanted me to let you know you are invited for dinner each night at the main house. She has dinner ready at six thirty."

"That sounds great. Tell her I said thank you."

"Will do. See you tonight then." He tipped his hat to her and was gone.

Torie could sense the stare of the woman working the cash register so she tried to push down the schoolgirl grin that fought its way to her face as she watched the door Keith had just exited.

She turned to the woman and smiled. The woman looked at the door then back at Torie. "That man is somethin' else, isn't he?" she said, chomping her gum. Her hair was streaked three different colors and was piled in a messy bun on top of her head.

Torie gave a non-committal, "Mmm-hmmm."

The woman shook her head. "There's not a woman around here that wouldn't want to call that man her own. But he won't even look at anyone. At least not until you." She eyed Torie over her glasses for a moment then stacked some papers on the counter and continued. "He's nice and polite and all, but...well, I'm not sure I'd trust another woman again either if I were him." She sighed. "Still wouldn't hurt for him to try though. There are nice girls around here that'd be good to him."

With that, she grabbed a stack of books and headed toward the travel section of the store.

Unsure of what just happened, Torie stood and stared. Why would Keith not trust women? She fought back the urge to defend him to the bookstore clerk. Whatever had happened to him in his past was his business. Not hers to share with some stranger in her store.

Torie shook her head. Small towns never change. She had firsthand knowledge of how hurtful small-town gossip could be, and it pained her to think of Keith wrapped up in any. She was curious, sure, but there was no way she'd ask him questions he didn't want to answer. The past was best buried. Another truth she knew all too well.

***

Keith found himself pacing the great room of the main house listening for Torie's truck in the drive. Sheesh. What was wrong with him? He was acting like a teenager hoping the pretty new girl in town would accept his invitation to dinner. Well, that wasn't far from the truth. But he was long gone from teen years and hadn't been this hyped over a woman since…well, he wasn't going there. Not tonight.

The sound of a car door slamming snapped him from his thoughts. She was here. She came. He could do this. Calm, cool, collected. He was a Marine, for crying out loud. He was control personified. The doorbell rang and he opened it. Torie stood there, her long, blond hair blowing in the breeze, and that was it. His palms were sweaty and his heart kicked up a notch. Her hazel eyes matched her long sweater. Black yoga pants hugged her mile-long legs then tucked into black Ugg boots. Her cheeks were rosy from the cold, without an ounce of makeup. She was the most beautiful creature he'd ever seen. A goddess right there on the front porch.

"Um, hey. Can I come in?"

Her voice broke him from his trance. He shook his head, hoping he didn't have drool on his face. Hell, this woman turned him inside out and upside down and he didn't have a clue what to do about it.

He stepped aside and ushered her into the house. "Yes. I'm sorry. It's freezing out there and you don't have a coat." Could he sound more like an idiot? He rubbed a hand down his face as he closed and locked the door.

Snap out of it, Scott. Be cool.

"I know. I forgot it when I left the cabin then figured I was just driving here and not walking so…" She shrugged and tucked a lock of stray hair behind her ear. Simple diamond studs adorned her earlobes. Beautiful. The kind of jewelry that could easily be a gift from a boyfriend. He hadn't even thought of that. Idiot. A woman like her must have men lined up at her door. The thought turned him green with envy but he pushed it down.

"Come sit by the fire. Dinner should be ready soon, but you can warm up until then."

"Thanks. That's perfect." She made her way through the great room and sat in a rocking chair next to the hearth.

"How about a warm drink?"

"Sounds great. Thank you."

Keith nodded and headed to the kitchen. He stopped in the hallway out of Torie's line of sight. He had to pull himself together. His mother would see in a hot second his interest in Torie. But who wouldn't? He'd acted like a love-struck teen just now when she came to the door. If he didn't snap out of it for dinner, his mother would have them choosing a wedding date by dessert. The fact that that idea didn't give Keith chills frightened him all the more.

When he'd first met Torie, she was all business, not afraid to stand up to him, tell him what she was thinking. And he liked her candor. But today he saw a softer side to her. She was the perfect mix of spicy and sweet. An enticing combination. No. Long-term relationships weren't for him. He took a deep breath. Right. Stick to the plan. Solider first. Everything else second. And Torie was definitely not a second place kind of woman. His resolve intact, he headed into the kitchen to get her a warm drink.

3

"I CAN'T THANK you enough for your invitation to dinner, Mrs. Scott," Torie said as she took a scoop from a heaping bowl of sweet potatoes then passed it on.

"Please, call me Ellie."

Keith's mother sat at one end of the dining table, his father at the other. He and Torie sat on each side, across from one another.

Colt and Ellie Scott were in their late fifties, having spent most of Keith's life as cattle ranchers. Starting their own ranch with some help from Keith's maternal grandparents, they'd built a strong business and one Keith was proud to help his father run. The 4S wasn't a working ranch, per se—their bread-and-butter ranch being in Texas. But his parents wanted a quiet, simple life in the mountains, so Tahoe fit them to a tee. With Dane helping out now too, the three men took turns traveling back and forth but trusted most of the operation to their foreman, who had worked with Colt since the beginning. It was a pace that fit Keith, one that balanced out his time in the service.

"I'm just so happy you agreed to join us, darlin'," his mother said to Torie. She winked at Keith, who had to fight the urge to roll his eyes. His mother was a matchmaker of epic proportions. Wanting grandchildren only stoked the fire. Maybe Dane and Aimee would have a honeymoon baby, helping take the pressure off of him. He smiled at the thought. Yeah, that would work.

"What are you grinning about?" Torie asked.

Oops. Caught.

"Nothin'." He tried to play it off, but the twinkle in his mother's eyes said it wasn't working.

Torie smirked at him and took a bite of steak. Lord help him, one look from her made him tingle all over.

"I'm surprised you're not spending Christmas with your family, Torie."

Keith's spine stiffened. Torie had been vague with him that morning about family, and he could sense something was off when it came to that subject. He watched Torie's body language for clues but she answered as calm as if his mother had asked where she shopped for clothing.

"I don't have family."

His mother looked at him and then back at Torie. She

would not understand the concept of no family, being one of six children and having a loving family dating back Lord knows how many centuries. His father as well. Family was everything to a Scott.

"You don't have family?" His father asked before his mother could.

No sir. My parents are gone and my gram is too. No siblings to speak of."

The three Scotts looked at one another and Torie avoided eye contact with them, the clank of her fork hitting her plate the only noise in the room.

"Well then." His mother broke the silence. "I'm glad you're here with us then." She sent her best southern smile Torie's direction.

God bless his mother. Her ability to make people feel at ease was a gift. Although she'd corner him later for sure and try to squeeze every ounce of info she could out of him. Not that he had any answers. Torie was as much a mystery to him as she was to his mother. A mystery that had captured his attention and wouldn't let go.

"How are you settling in to the cabin, Torie? I hope you're comfortable there." His father, too, had a knack for knowing when a subject change was best.

"It's lovely, thank you for asking. I can't imagine anyone not being able to make themselves at home there. Dane and Aimee did a beautiful job."

"Yes they did," his mother agreed. "Keith did most of

the renovations for them since it was a hush, hush situation." She winked at Torie.

Dane and Aimee had planned their wedding for the week before Christmas, but a month before that decided to elope instead. They still went through with the bigger ceremony as planned but moved into their cabin weeks before Aimee was expecting to. Dane roped Keith into helping him get the cabin ready, wanting it to be a surprise for his bride. He didn't mind. He liked Aimee. Was glad she and Dane found one another. He was happy for his little brother. He'd found something…someone…Keith would never find.

"I didn't realize you were such a handyman." Torie's teasing brought him from his thoughts.

"Oh yes," his mother answered for him. "He loves to build things. Always has. As a little boy, I think he played with Lincoln Logs more than anything else. Little towns used to line the hallways…"

"Mom." Keith cut her off before she could get to how easy he was to potty train or that he slept with a nightlight until he was eight. He still had to sleep with the hall light on, but that wasn't something he was about to share either. And now it was for completely different reasons.

Torie's giggle floated through the air, filling him with warmth. Her eyes sparkled as she watched him from across the table, the napkin she held in front of her mouth doing nothing to hide her grin. She was enjoying this, the evil woman.

Keith smiled. How could he not? "Yes. I like to build things. And no, I didn't mind helping my brother in his time of need."

"I heard you helped in other ways too."

If Torie kept looking at him that way he just might have to come around to her side of the table and kiss that perfect mouth she had curved into a smile.

Keith cleared his throat. "I may have helped put some flowers around and light the fireplace for him the day they eloped, yes, but that was it."

"Such a romantic buried in that big tough Captain America exterior." Torie laughed.

Keith couldn't take his eyes off Torie, but he could sure feel the look his mother was giving them. Torie's teasing brought visions of grandchildren dancing in Ellie's head, for sure. And for the first time in years, he didn't mind it one bit.

He was in trouble. Six-foot blonde with hazel eyes kind of trouble.

* * *

After dinner the four of them sat in the great room in front of a roaring fire. There were vaulted ceilings made of knotty pine and a stone fireplace that went from floor to ceiling. Bookshelves flanked the fireplace with flowers, books, knick-knacks, and family photos. All the furniture was big and inviting. Torie was sunk down in a chair, her feet propped up on an ottoman and a blanket over her legs. Ellie had insisted and Torie hadn't fought her on it. She hadn't been pampered like that since she lived with Gram, another lifetime ago.

Keith sat on one end of the sofa. He chatted with his dad about horses, and Torie soaked in the atmosphere. This was a home. A loving one. She could sense how kindness from its inhabitants had seeped into the walls. Every room bore evidence of laughter and love, welcoming all who entered. As she sipped her decaf coffee and watched the flames flicker in the fireplace, she embraced the warmth of the moment. It wouldn't last. It wouldn't last because it wasn't hers to have. She'd never had a loving family and she never would. As welcoming as the Scotts were, they were their own entity and she was an outsider. Like always.

Tears fought their way out, but she'd be damned if she'd let them fall. She'd been on her own a long time. That was familiar. A known factor. She swallowed her tears with another sip of coffee and turned her attention back towards Keith and his parents. Digging down deep she found her best beauty pageant smile, taught from day one by her mother, and pushed down any thoughts of family. She'd done it time and time again. She could certainly do it now.

Her smile faded, however, when her mind floated back into the conversation.

"Oh yes, dear. You need a Christmas tree over there. Keith can help you with one."

"I'm sorry, what?" Torie needed to catch up with the line

of conversation before she agreed to anything.

"My wife was just saying you should put up a Christmas tree at the cabin," Colt said.

"Oh. Right. No. That's okay. I don't want anyone to go to any trouble."

"It wouldn't be any trouble at all, dear. Would it, Keith?" Ellie looked at her son with promise. The woman was relentless.

Torie still had to try. "Really. It's fine. If I want to enjoy a tree I'll just come over here. Yours is lovely." She pointed to the Blue Spruce that had to be fifteen feet tall and stood in front of the floor-to-ceiling windows that looked out over the backyard. An electric train ran around the bottom. Nativity scenes, white cotton snow with sleighs and reindeer adorned every flat surface in the room. The entire great room looked like Santa's workshop.

"Oh pish-posh. You'll have a tree. Keith can get you one tomorrow, right, Son?"

"Sure, Mom. I'll get her a tree."

Keith nodded at his mother and smiled at Torie. She tried to return the sentiment but failed. Instead, she put her coffee mug to her mouth and turned again to the fire.

She didn't have anything against Christmas trees. It was the holiday itself she tried to avoid altogether. The merriment and gift giving wasn't something she'd spent a lot of time enjoying when she was young, and they were usually too poor to have a tree. Her mother had tried for a few years but eventually gave up. It wasn't worth the fight.

"Oh, and Keith," Ellie continued, "don't forget, our annual Christmas party is this weekend, so I'll need your help getting that set up."

"Sure, Mom. Just let me know what you need."

"And we would love to have you here for that as well, Torie." Ellie looked at her for a response. The woman was joy personified. She made it nearly impossible to say no to her.

"That sounds great." Torie said it but wasn't sure she meant it. She liked to party as much as the next girl, but a Christmas party with strangers didn't sound too appealing. It was days away though, so she could probably get out of it. However, with Ellie Scott involved, that wasn't likely.

It was time for her to go.

"I better get back."

The three of them stood as she did, Ellie taking her coffee mug from her and taking it to the kitchen. Torie busied herself with folding the blanket, anything to avoid Keith's eyes. He hadn't said much to her since dinner, but she sure felt his gaze on her the entire evening. It warmed her and flustered her all at the same time. Having some fun with Keith would be great, but she didn't do long term. Life was safer that way. And she didn't get a "just out for fun" kind of vibe from him.

Yes. Best to keep it lighthearted like she always did with men.

"Let me walk you out." Keith's baritone voice sent a tingle down her spine. She could keep things light.

Right. And Santa would be bringing her a million dollars for Christmas.

* * *

Keith pulled his truck up next to Torie's. He'd insisted on following her back to the cabin, make sure she was tucked in and safe. She could handle herself, for sure, but the gesture warmed her anyway. Men didn't tend to want to take care of her. Something she'd made peace with long ago. But it didn't hurt to have a little extra watching over right now either. There was a slim chance anyone would find her here, but knowing Keith was looking out for her was comforting.

The moon cast a soft glow over the meadow surrounding the place. It was a cold, clear night. Stars filled the sky. Crickets chirped. Worlds away from a big city. Torie sighed. Someday. Someday, maybe she could live in a place like this.

They hopped out of their vehicles and walked to the front porch.

"Sorry about my mom. I know she can be kind of pushy sometimes. She means well though." Keith had his hands in his jean pockets. He shuffled his boot over a wood plank of the porch, the gesture making him look like a young boy. Humorous, really, considering the size of the man.

"I know. She's a sweetheart. And there's nothing wrong with her wanting me to have a nice Christmas. It's thoughtful of her, and I hope I didn't seem ungrateful. That last thing I'd ever want to do is hurt her feelings."

"It's all good. Like I said, she means well. If you don't want a tree, just say so. She'll get over it."

"No. No. A tree would be… great. I don't have anything to decorate it with though."

"Don't worry. I'm sure Mom has that covered as well." His attempt to sound irritated with his mom fell flat. She was amazing and he knew it.

"I'll bet she does." Torie laughed.

He shrugged. "She loves Christmas."

Torie could only nod. What was there to say? Everyone loved Christmas, right? That was the assumption, anyway. She really didn't want to hurt Ellie's feelings. Having a Christmas tree wouldn't be so bad. It wouldn't change anything.

"How does tomorrow afternoon sound? To go tree shopping?"

"Sounds great. Thanks." She looked out at their trucks and back again. "You didn't have to follow me here. It's not like I'm staying in a bad neighborhood or anything." She smiled up at him.

"I realize that. But I was raised to be a gentleman, you see." He gave her a dimpled grin that caused a shiver to run through her.

"Speaking of, you must be freezing. Here." He took off his coat and wrapped it around her, holding the front together just below the collar. It almost swallowed her whole. She closed her eyes and breathed in the scent of pine and leather and male.

Keith.

She opened her eyes as he leaned forward and placed a kiss on her cheek. His stubble brushed against her skin, sending goose bumps down her arms. He lingered a moment, kissing her once more.

"Good night, Torie," he whispered in her ear. He straightened and winked at her. "I'll pick you up tomorrow around three and we'll get you that Christmas tree."

Dumbstruck, all she could do was nod.

He sauntered down the porch toward his truck. With a nod of his Stetson, he got in and drove away, leaving her on the porch wrapped in his coat, her hand touching her skin where he'd kissed her.

4

TORIE SAT ON the sofa, staring at the fireplace. She'd tossed and turned all night thinking about Keith. Going for a run early that morning to try and get her head back on straight hadn't worked. The novel she'd bought at the bookstore sat open and facedown in her lap. She'd begun reading it, hoping for a distraction, but after noticing she hadn't retained a word of the past few pages, she gave up. That wasn't working either.

She went back and forth between wanting three o'clock to arrive and not wanting it to, simply because she was unsure how she'd handle herself around Keith. He'd kissed her cheek and she'd felt it all the way to her toes. If he ever truly kissed her she might just faint.

When she first arrived at the 4S Ranch, it was for Dane and Aimee's wedding. Throughout the festivities, Keith had been quiet, mainly kept to himself. It became obvious crowds weren't his thing. But in the past few days she'd seen a side to him beyond the big, bad soldier-boy image he didn't seem to mind portraying. And she liked it. Truthfully, she liked both sides. A lot.

Nerves did a little dance in her tummy. She wanted to spend time with Keith, very much so, but wasn't sure she was ready to visit Christmas past or explain why she never had a tree. It wasn't as if she'd *never* had a good Christmas. The years with Gram were good. Simple, but good. Gram couldn't afford much, but would still find a way to give Torie something. A favorite book that had been hers as a girl, a knitted scarf. And every year, Gram would read the Christmas story from the Bible. Torie would sit at her feet and listen with rapt attention about the baby born to save the world. She loved that story. But like most stories, it was too good to be true. Jesus may have come to save the world, but she was beyond saving.

And it's not like Torie'd never, ever had a Christmas tree in her house. For heaven's sake, living with Aimee was like living with an eternal little kid. She'd decorate the apartment each year but still, come Christmas Eve and Christmas morning, Aimee was with her family. Torie was at work.

The sound of Keith's truck outside brought her back to the present. She placed her book on the coffee table and kicked the blanket off her legs. Triple-checking herself in the mirror, she took a deep breath. "It's not a date, Walker. He's helping you get a tree. No big deal."

That's what her mind said. Her fluttering heartbeat didn't seem to agree.

* * *

Keith parked his truck next to Torie's outside Dane and Aimee's cabin. He'd never peg her to be the type to drive an old Ford truck, 2002 if he took a guess, but nothing about Torie made sense. She had the look of a runway model but worked as a cop. She had an underlying tenderness that for whatever reason, she guarded with a tough exterior. To keep people out? To protect herself? But protect herself from what—or maybe who? The desire to know nudged his insides.

He'd observed her after dinner at his parents' house the night before. Curled up under a blanket in a big chair by the fire, her body language said contentment. But her eyes said something else. She'd put up a brave front when his mother hounded her about a Christmas tree, fake smiles and all, but loneliness clouded the hazel depths of her eyes. And Keith wanted nothing more than for her to look at him and know she didn't have to be alone. Not for this holiday anyway.

·Last night as he drove away from the cabin, he'd glanced in his rearview mirror and the image of her wrapped in his coat, her hand on her cheek, warmed him the rest of the evening. He hadn't meant to kiss her. He wanted, no needed, to keep his distance. Keep it friendly. But she'd looked at him with those lonely eyes of hers, and the strength of a thousand horses couldn't have held him back.

And hell, a simple kiss on her cheek had sent a fire through him. What might happen if he actually kissed those lips of hers? He shook his head and patted Bones who sat beside him looking at him as if to say, "We're here. What are we waiting for?"

"Excellent question, girl. Let's go see a lady about a tree."

Keith climbed out of his truck, Bones jumping down behind him and trotting over to Torie, who stood on the front porch.

"Hey girl! I didn't know you were joining us today." Torie squatted down and rubbed Bones behind her ears. Bones gave her best happy panting doggy smile.

"I hope you don't mind. She likes to join in whenever possible."

"It's absolutely fine. I'm so glad you brought her." Torie leaned in towards the dog, who was more than happy to kiss Torie right on the nose. Torie giggled.

Lucky dog.

* * *

"You ready?" Keith asked.

"Yep. Let's do this." Torie walked to the passenger side of Keith's truck where he'd gone around to hold the door open for her. She thanked him and climbed in. Bones hopped in on his side and sat between them.

They bounced down the dirt road, Rascal Flatts singing on the radio about wishing to rewind the perfect night, experience it all over again. It was chilly out, but the sun warmed them through the windshield. Bones's fur was soft under Torie's hand as she rubbed the dog's back. Keith hummed to the music.

Whatever potential weirdness she worried about with him today after last night was gone. Contentment filled the cab of the truck and Torie soaked it in. She couldn't remember the last time she felt this comfortable with a man. She'd dated, sure, but that was different. That was putting on her best smile and keeping things light. Nothing felt light with Keith. Not heavy either. Things with him were…comfortable. Safe. She let her guard down and was herself. Sheesh, she hadn't even put on makeup since she got here.

Keith's humming filled the cab of his truck. Torie smiled.

"What?"

"I didn't say anything."

"You were smiling at me."

"Was I?" She teased. "I just didn't see you as a…humming sort of guy."

A deep chuckle shook him and a dimpled grin peeked out from under his pulled-down Stetson. "Oh really? Do I want to know what a humming sort of guy looks like?"

She shrugged and continued to stroke Bones's fur. "I'm not saying it's bad. It's…nice, actually. Calming." She laid her head back against the seat and closed her eyes.

"You okay?"

"Mmmm-hmmmm. Never better." She meant it too.

Feeling his eyes on her, she opened hers and looked at him. "My world is pretty intense. I didn't realize until I got here how often I don't…"

"Don't what?" His gaze intensified then turned to watch the road.

"Let go, I guess."

"What are you holding on to?"

"I guess that's the million dollar question, isn't it?"

He put his hand on top of the one that sat on Bones's neck, continuing to guide his truck with the other. He didn't say anything. Just held her hand. No pat answer, no more questions.

Choking back tears, she turned again towards the window. Tahoe was so beautiful. Earth tones and snow white streaked by—so many colors.

Keith's thumb rubbed across her knuckles, the tenderness of the gesture warming her insides. They rode the rest of the way in silence, and for the first time since Gram died, Torie didn't feel alone.

* * *

"We're here."

Keith parked his truck in the dirt lot. He came around

and opened Torie's door for her, Bones climbing out behind and trotting around to sit by his feet.

"Where are we?" Torie asked.

"A Christmas tree farm."

"Huh. Okay."

Keith had no idea what Torie's past was like but he was beginning to grasp it wasn't good. He'd guessed right when thinking she probably had never gone and chopped down her own tree before. The look on her face said it all. Confused, unsure, and a little intrigued.

"You ever cut down your own tree before?" He reached in the bed of his truck and pulled out a large saw.

Her eyes grew wide. "Um. No."

He laughed. "It's okay. I have. This is gonna be fun." He winked at her and took her hand, guiding her towards the trees. Rows and rows of them, side by side, in all shapes and sizes. The farm had a small covered area where people could borrow saws if they didn't bring their own. Alan Jackson sang about letting it be Christmas from a stereo system behind the counter where clerks were taking money for trees. Keith paid the fee then guided Torie through the front gate. Bones trotted happily beside them.

Keith stopped halfway up the first row and turned towards Torie. Arms spread out wide, he said, "Take your pick, my lady. Any one of these is yours. Just tell me which one and I'll chop it down for you." He pointed to the saw in his hand.

Torie looked at the saw and then at him. "Seriously?"

"Seriously."

Her bright eyes glistened the color of a plush meadow on a spring day and she giggled. Keith's body tingled all the way to his toes at the sound.

"Okay!" She wrapped her coat around her and looked around. "I don't know where to start."

"Well, do you like a full, plush tree or one that's maybe lighter, a little more sparse?"

Her smile faded a bit. "I'm...not sure."

Right. She hadn't done this before.

If Keith wanted to make this a good memory for her, he had to stay focused. Not get lost in her hair that cascaded down over her camel-colored coat like a golden waterfall. Or those eyes that mesmerized him.

"Let's just start walking and you let me know if something catches your eye."

He took her hand again and led her down the path, keeping her near trees whose size would work in the cabin. Nothing too tall or too wide, but definitely her perfect Christmas tree. Everything in him wanted to give her that.

She pulled back on his hand and stopped. "That one is pretty." He turned to look where she pointed.

"Yes it is. But you've gotta check it from all sides."

She nodded. "Okay."

She walked around it, looking it up and down. "No. Let's keep looking."

He nodded and followed as she took a turn and tried a different row of trees. After a while he noticed she liked fuller, plush trees, just like he did. She'd narrowed it down to two and was looking back and forth, trying to decide.

He watched as she eyed both trees. At one point she ran her teeth along her bottom lip, deep in thought. At that moment he wanted nothing more than to kiss those lips.

"That one!"

Her excitement brought him from his thoughts. Which was a good thing. He needed to keep his cool.

His eyes followed Torie's pointing finger. "That's an excellent choice."

"You think?"

He chuckled. "I do. Let's get this cut down and back to the cabin for you to decorate."

Her face lit up and she grinned from ear to ear. "You're right. This is fun."

Keith smiled back then knelt to cut down the tree. He pulled gloves from his pocket and put them on. Only about a six-footer and not super wide, it didn't take him long to cut his way through. Handing Torie the saw, he picked up the tree and headed to his truck. She followed behind, Bones trotting along beside them.

Keith placed the tree and saw into the bed of his truck. He took off his gloves and tossed them in as well.

"You want some hot chocolate?"

He loved how Torie's eyes lit up once again. Man, he'd

move heaven and earth to make that happen time and time again.

"Sure. That sounds great."

They walked back to the small entrance of the tree farm where a young teenage girl stood behind a counter selling hot chocolate. Three picnic tables sat nearby. Keith paid for two hot chocolates and handed one to Torie.

"There you go, ma'am."

"Thank you, kind sir." She smiled up at him as she took a sip. Her hands wrapped around the paper cup to soak in the heat.

Keith took a sip, letting the chocolate sit on his tongue a moment before swallowing. The cool air and Christmas music mixed with the sweetness in his mouth made a perfect combination of holiday cheer. But nothing matched the joy that radiated from Torie. He didn't know what she meant before about holding on too tight, but he was glad she had let go today. With him. More and more he wanted to make her smile. Make her feel safe enough to let go. But would she let him? And was he willing to take a chance again?

He looked down at her, now hunched over to pet Bones. The dog licked her cheek. His heart still longed for another chance at forever, but he wasn't sure it could survive another break.

She looked up at him and smiled, a small drop of chocolate on her chin.

Oh yeah, she could break his heart. But man, for the first

time in years, he was considering it worth the risk.

She stood and took another sip of cocoa. A second drop landed on her chin. With a smile, he reached out and swept his thumb across, wiping the drops away. She laughed and looked away, embarrassed. They sipped their drinks and watched as families tied Christmas trees to the tops of minivans, kids jumping happily around their parents. One couple placed a tiny tree in the trunk of their car then kissed like newlyweds. A young couple headed to their first apartment to decorate and celebrate their first holiday together, Keith guessed.

"Hey you two," the young teen girl said, pulling Keith's attention from people watching. "You're under the mistletoe."

He looked up and then at Torie, whose cheeks had turned a deep shade of red.

"That we are," Keith said, answering the young girl. But his eyes never left Torie's.

He took the cup from her hands and placed their hot chocolates on the table nearby.

"I would hate to be one to break from tradition," he whispered, taking her face in his hands and placing his lips to hers.

Her mouth was warmth and softness and chocolate. A combination that left his mind spinning and his body on fire. He didn't linger long. As much as he wanted to stay there for hours, maybe days, his need to be cautious won out. He pulled back and looked into her eyes, now a smoky green.

She smiled. "Traditions are nice…"

"Yes. Yes they are." He stepped back, putting some space between them, instantly missing the connection.

Bones pawed at Torie's leg. Huh. Guess he wasn't the only one who'd taken a liking to Torie. She patted Bones on the head and scratched behind her ears. The dog had the nerve to look at him with blissful eyes as if to say, "See, she likes me best."

"You finished?" Torie asked holding up their cups.

"Yeah. Thanks."

She took them to a trashcan nearby and tossed them. On her way back to Keith she walked right through a huge mud puddle, mucking both boots almost to the ankle.

"Ugh! Seriously?"

Keith couldn't help it. One look at her standing there, both feet buried in mud, arms out to the sides and her nose scrunched in disgust, and he lost it. Laughter from deep down worked its way out to where his body shook and his stomach hurt. It gripped him so hard he had to lean forward on his knees.

"Ha, ha. Very funny, Captain America. I'm glad you're entertained."

He stood and took a long breath. "Oh, man. Thank you. I haven't laughed like that in I don't know how long!"

Torie glared at him, only making her look more beautiful, if that was even possible.

Without a second thought he strolled over, bent down, hoisted her over his shoulder, and headed to his truck.

"What the....? What are you doing?"

Her shrieks came from the vicinity of his lower back and she kicked her legs. "Hey now. Quit fussin' or you'll get us both all muddy. I'm helping."

"*This* is helping?" She was still perturbed, but at least she'd stopped kicking.

"I got you out of the puddle and I'm escorting you to the truck. Yes, I'd call that helpful."

A grunt from over his shoulder was all he heard as he made his way across the parking lot. Bones hopped and nipped at Torie, who hung across his shoulder like a doll.

Keith laughed. He wasn't too sure if this day would be a good memory for Torie. He hoped so. But it was for a fact, one of the best days he'd had in a long time.

5

TORIE WATCHED AS Keith lifted the tree from his truck and placed it by the front porch as if it hardly weighed anything. He walked back and pulled a tree stand and the saw from the truck bed.

Unsure of how to help, Torie stood on the porch and watched, patting Bones, who sat next to her, as Keith began to cut the trunk of the tree to a size that would fit the stand. She took a moment to appreciate the muscles working to make sure the tree she chose stood just right. She'd gotten an up close and personal feel of said muscles when he'd tossed her over his shoulder. Not that she was complaining. It had shocked her at first, for sure, but once she'd settled in, it was a mighty nice ride, muddy boots and all.

And the kiss under the mistletoe? She'd have to file that

one away to think about later, because the mix of *that* man and chocolate was a lethal combination. Good Lord, the man could kiss. She figured as much after last night, having her cheek tingle at his touch. But the reality versus her imagination won out big time.

His dark brown coat stretched across his back as he moved the saw back and forth. She thought of the coat he'd wrapped around her the night before and knew she needed to return it. But if she were honest, she'd stayed wrapped up in it long after he'd left and wasn't quite ready to part with it yet. A little high schoolish of her, yes, but so what?

"Um, can I help somehow?" As much as she enjoyed standing there ogling Keith, she didn't like the idea of him doing all the work for her.

He looked over his shoulder at her. "There's a box of ornaments and such in the back of the truck. You wanna grab those?"

She nodded and did as he asked. The box was enormous but she was able to get a grip on it and bring it to the porch. "Let me guess, Ellie had some extras."

He laughed and stood. "Told ya. Come on. Let's get this inside."

Torie unlocked the front door and moved aside as Keith brought in the tree. She'd made a spot for it that morning in the corner of the room to the left of the fireplace. Keith set it down and got to work on getting it straight in the stand while Torie dragged the box of decorations inside.

"Bones is sitting outside the door staring and wagging her tail."

Keith's voice came from under the tree where he was now lying down, his face hidden under the branches and his long legs sticking out while he screwed the bolts into the trunk. "She won't come inside unless I tell her to."

"It's fine with me if she's in here." Torie looked between him and the dog, whose ears perked and head tilted. Keith gave a quick whistle and Bones trotted inside and parked herself on the rug in front of the fireplace as if that was where she belonged.

"Wow. One little whistle and she just does what you say, huh?" Torie teased.

"I have that kind of effect on females," Keith quipped back.

Torie laughed. Oh, she had no doubt that was true. She watched as Keith guided the tree into place.

"Is it straight?" His muffled voice came through the branches.

Torie stood in the center of the room and looked. "A little to the left."

"K." More shuffling of branches. "Better?"

"Yeah. That's good."

The tree shook a bit more as he secured the screws to stabilize the tree. Having never really done this, a sense of vulnerability washed over Torie and she didn't like it. She'd spent years making sure she was always in control of a situation. New experiences weren't really her thing. And new experiences with gorgeous men who made her heart race and her palms sweat she wasn't too sure about either. Uncomfortable didn't begin to describe the moment.

Keith crawled out from under the tree and stood next to her. He'd tossed his hat on the table near the door before maneuvering the tree into the corner. A sprig of pine stuck out of what little hair he had on top of his head. Torie smiled. Yet another glimpse behind the mountain of man to the sweet boy he must have been.

He caught her staring. "What? What is it?"

She smiled up at him. "You have a twig stuck..." She reached up and pulled it out for him then smoothed his hair where it had poked up. The gesture was meant to be friendly but the heat she saw in his eyes matched what surged through her system.

He cleared his throat and stepped back. "Thank you."

"Sure." She tried to keep her voice from cracking but failed. "Thank you for doing all of this." She motioned to the box of decorations. "I'm afraid I'm a tad out of my element here though. We didn't do this much...if at all when I was a kid."

"Well..." He moved toward the box. "You have to put the lights on first. Then the ornaments." He reached in and pulled out a string of colored lights. "Do you prefer white lights or colors?"

She hesitated. Just stared at him and then the string of

lights in his hand. "Um, white I guess."

He smiled. "Me too. The white lights shine through the ornaments and light them up better than the colors, in my opinion."

Torie liked how he asked her what she wanted then shared what he preferred. He didn't try and sway her one way or the other, just let her decide. She'd never had someone who honestly cared what she thought or what she wanted. A small part of her was glad he liked the same.

He shrugged out of his coat and laid it on the back of the sofa. He rolled up his shirtsleeves and dove once more into the box. "Here's a few strings of white. I'm sure my mom has already checked, but let's plug them in to make sure they work." He handed them to Torie. "Why don't you do that and I'll get a nice fire going in the fireplace for us."

Torie nodded and took the lights from him, mesmerized by the power and strength showcased in his forearms. She turned away and shook her head, if only to rattle loose the fantasies in her head. She was never one to wig out over a man. Why was she all but drooling over Keith now? She busied herself with finding an outlet to plug the lights in. Yes. That was a good idea. Stay focused.

She squatted down and plugged in one strand and then another. The floor lit up where the lights sat coiled together. A giggle escaped her. Slowly, one by one, the lights began to dance, flickering like lightning bugs along the floor.

"They work!" she shouted to Keith, now stacking wood

in the fireplace. "And they twinkle!"

* * *

Keith's pulse quickened as he turned to look at Torie. The Christmas lights she'd just plugged in lit up her face and sheer joy danced in her eyes. Her hair hung in golden waves, framing her face like an angel. He'd never seen anything more beautiful in his entire life.

She knelt on the floor, now holding a clump of lights in her hands, watching them as if they held magic within. Sheesh. She never had experienced Christmas, had she? His heart broke at what must have been a painful growing up for her. He'd never known anything but love and magical holidays. Things that were so easy to take for granted.

She giggled again, the sound bubbling into the air and warming his insides. "Pretty cool, isn't it?" He turned back to light the fire, if only to give himself a moment to pull himself together. If he kept watching her, he just might risk falling for her. Something he couldn't afford to do and something he wouldn't put her through.

Who was he kidding? He could tell himself until he was blue in the face he didn't have feelings for Torie. But it wouldn't be the first time he'd lied to himself to avoid pain.

"Okay. What's next?" Torie's excitement was palpable.

"Well, why don't we find some Christmas music to play?" Keith kicked himself as the words left his mouth. Christmas music was just what they needed to add to the romantic scene unfolding before them.

Right. He was doing a bang up job of avoiding feelings for Torie.

"Oh. Okay. Sure."

He turned back to her, the fire now catching and building in the fireplace. She stood behind the sofa, her fingers toying with the blanket that lay across the back.

There was a small speaker system sitting on top of the cabinet in the corner of the room. An iPod was perched on top. "I'll check out Dane's iPod. I'm sure there's something. Why don't you go through the box and start pulling out ornaments?" His suggestion had the desired effect, her eyes lighting up again as she came around the sofa and stood over the box, peering inside as if the secrets of the universe were inside.

Mission accomplished. She was back in Christmas magic mode.

Keith thumbed through the iPod and chose a mix labeled "Christmas." He sent up a silent thank-you to Dane and Aimee. Lady Antebellum began singing about all they wanted for Christmas and the room filled with warmth from the fire as well as the music.

He joined Torie as she pulled a shoebox from the larger box and sat on the sofa to open it. She unwrapped the ornaments carefully and held each one up to see before setting them carefully on the coffee table in front of her. A tiny reindeer with a red nose, a Santa with a big belly that jiggled when the ornament moved, a sleigh that said "Scott Family" across the side.

"Keith, these are so beautiful. I can't believe your mom is okay to part with these. Why aren't they on her tree in the main house?"

He chuckled. "You've seen my mother's tree in the main house, right?"

Torie nodded.

"Need I say more?"

She laughed in understanding. Ellie's tree was jammed full of ornaments. Trying to put one more on would cause the tree to topple for sure.

"I guess you're right," Torie said as she unwrapped another ornament as if it were the most precious thing she'd ever held in her life. "That tree is pretty full. I guess she can spare these."

They worked in quiet from that point on as Keith wound the lights around the tree and Torie dug through the ornaments some more. Her inner child emerged again when she found the boxes of multi-colored Christmas balls.

Keith watched her in awe. He'd never seen someone experience Christmas, truly experience it, for the very first time. Before meeting Torie he couldn't even have imagined that was possible. Sure, he'd seen the worst kind of evil and destruction that comes with fighting in war, but nothing tore at his heart like the thought of Torie not having the kind of love he'd known his entire existence. That love was part of what kept him going when he was overseas. What helped keep him alive. He had his family to come home to.

His heart sank. He'd had more to come home to at one point in time. But that was long gone. He couldn't let his heart go there. Not now. Today had been perfect. One of the best days since…well, since as long as he could remember. No matter what had happened to him, Torie didn't have anyone. His mind couldn't wrap around the concept.

They finished hanging the ornaments and Keith let Torie put the star on top of the tree. The final piece.

With the mess of pine needles cleaned up and the box from his mom, now empty, stored in Dane and Aimee's bedroom, they sat side by side on the sofa, admiring their work.

"It's so beautiful." Torie's words were a reverent whisper.

Keith had turned off all the other lights, and with the sun going down, the room was almost completely dark around them. The tree shone like a beacon in the corner. Shadows danced off the walls and ceiling as the lights twinkled.

He looked at Torie. The lights flickered off her eyes, the hazel depths glowing.

"I'm sorry you've never gotten to do this."

She blinked and looked at him. "It's okay." She tried to shrug it away but it wasn't okay. He'd seen it in how she marveled at everything they'd done that day. From chopping down the tree until this moment, soaking in the wonder the color and lights brought to the dark room.

The fire crackled in the fireplace. Keith settled back into the couch, appreciating the way he could sit in quiet with Torie without it feeling strange. He'd never had that with a woman. Not even Mandy. He pushed down any thought of her. No way would he let his past ruin this time with Torie.

"I'm glad I got to do this with you."

Her voice was a whisper he barely heard. He didn't answer. Just looked at her.

She sighed then turned back to the tree. "As you may have guessed, my childhood wasn't a fun one."

He still didn't speak. Just waited for her to continue, if she wanted to.

She did. "My dad was abusive and my mom...she died when I was fourteen." Her voice choked but no tears fell. "I went to live with my gram. She was awesome. The years I was with her were the best of my life. We didn't have a lot, but she made me feel loved. I hadn't had a whole lot of that before then."

Keith took her hand and held it between them on the sofa. He needed to touch her. Comfort her in some way. Reassure her that she mattered. Hell if he knew why, but it was the truth of the moment.

She smiled, never looking away from the tree. She rested her head on his shoulder and sighed. Oh yeah, this was the best day of his life so far. Torie had tilted his world on its axis when she sauntered into his life a few months ago, but right now, at this moment, the world was perfect.

6

TORIE LAY IN bed and looked up at the ceiling. The guest room in the cabin was upstairs. The ceiling was made of huge logs criss-crossing, a lantern hanging from the center with dangling lamps all around. A stone fireplace adorned the corner and a picture window along the other wall had a small bench Torie liked to sit on and look outside. The forest and trees beyond were always so peaceful.

Her thoughts wandered to last night. Who was she kidding? Her thoughts had been on last night since Keith kissed her cheek at the door and wished her sweet dreams. How could her dreams not be sweet? They were filled with him.

He'd been so amazing the night before, letting her talk and simply listening. He didn't push her to say more and yet she found herself talking about her parents and Gram, something she hadn't even done with Aimee, who she considered her best friend. Torie snuggled deeper in the covers and sighed. Everything about Keith made her feel safe. When they'd first met, Aimee talked about how big and imposing he was, but he wasn't, not to Torie. His presence brought comfort.

Her phone dinged on the nightstand. Maybe it was Keith. Grinning like a schoolgirl, she reached over and grabbed her phone. Her smile faded, however, when she saw who had left a voice mail. It wasn't Keith.

Her pulse sped up as she stared at the screen. Part of her wanted to hear the message, get the information she needed, and move on. Another part of her wanted to close her eyes and dream again of Keith.

She took a deep breath and tapped play on her voice mail. The deep voice coming through the speaker overtook the peace of the room.

"Hey, Torie. It's Frank. I'm afraid I don't have good news. Due to a technicality, he made parole. He's set to meet with his parole officer tomorrow. You and I both know that's highly unlikely, so watch your back. I'll keep you posted."

Torie's gut twisted as her phone slipped from her hand and landed on the comforter. This couldn't be happening. A technicality? How the…..? She shook her head and wiped a stray tear that had worked its way down her cheek. She had to get out of the house. Do something. Have somewhere for her adrenaline to go.

She hopped out of bed and changed into her workout clothes and shoes. Throwing her hair in a ponytail, she left the cabin and started jogging down the trail that led from Dane and Aimee's place to the main house. With each step, her fear faded a bit and the sense of control she craved returned. It also cleared her head. So he made parole. Okay. That wasn't the end of the world. Yet. Maybe he would meet with his parole officer and behave. Follow the rules. For once. It was a big maybe, but she had to stay clear headed until she knew exactly what she was dealing with.

The path curved and the barn came into view. She'd loved horses as a kid and saw plenty of them living with Gram in Wyoming, but she'd never ridden one. Curious, she made her way up to the small door at the back of the barn and poked her head in. Expecting to see horse stalls and riding tack, she was surprised to find the back end of the barn had been turned into a workout room, complete with a full weight system, pull-up bar, and miscellaneous workout gear.

"No way," she whispered. It was like her own private playground dropped from the sky just for her. Stress relief heaven.

She closed the door behind her and looked around. Surely the Scotts wouldn't mind her using their "gym" while she was here. What was that phrase? Sometimes it's better to ask for forgiveness than for permission?

She unclipped her iPod from her hip and unplugged her

headphones. Turning up the music, she set the iPod on a nearby hay bale and got started. This was exactly what she needed. A good workout to get her focused again. Remind her she wasn't the frail kid afraid of the world anymore. She was stronger than that. Tougher. She grabbed a twenty-pound medicine ball and got to work.

* * *

Keith made his way toward the barn. He'd tossed and turned all night thinking about Torie. A cool shower this morning hadn't help matters so he figured a good, long workout would get his mind off her. At least for a little while.

It wasn't as if there was anything wrong with Torie. In fact, it was the opposite. He couldn't remember the last time he'd sat on a sofa with a woman and just...hung out. He wasn't much of a talker to begin with, and most women he met were. But not Torie. Sure, she'd told him about her family, something he sensed wasn't easy for her. She was beginning to trust him and he liked that. He liked that a lot. But most of the evening they sat in peaceful silence, appreciating the tree and listening to music.

It also wasn't easy to tamp down his attraction to Torie, but when she said her dad had been abusive, some things fell into place. And the last thing Keith wanted was to scare her away. Trusting him couldn't be easy for her and the fact that Torie *did* made him even more protective of her than he already was.

He shook his head. What was he thinking? Getting any closer to Torie was not a good idea. They were just friends, right? He could do that. Be friends. His head said that was the way to go. His heart chuckled and said, "Just keep telling yourself that one, Dude."

The barn came into view. Good. Time to get a good sweat going and his mind off Torie. He stopped. Was that music coming from the barn? He moved towards the door. Yep. Someone was in there. And playing '60s music.

Keith opened the door and peered inside. The music came from an iPod propped up on a hay bale. A discarded T-shirt lay nearby. What the....? This was his private oasis from the world. Who would be using it without his permission?

Soft grunts caused him to turn his head. All hope of forgetting about Torie flew out the window. Dressed in workout clothes that showed every curve, she was doing pull-ups like her life depended on it. She was six feet of pure muscle. Solid on the outside, shattered and frail on the inside.

Good Lord, he was in trouble.

She hadn't seen him yet. He stood in the doorway a moment more and watched, not wanting to scare her and also wanting a moment to compose himself. She knocked him off his game on every level.

She dropped from the pull-up bar and immediately went to push-ups. Crap, this woman was intense. He'd seen women in the Marine Corps who could run circles around some of the men but still... Torie was a force to be reckoned with, physically and otherwise.

The song ended on her iPod and the quiet in the barn was palpable, her heavy breathing the only sound. He took a step inside the door and the crackle of hay beneath his feet caused her to turn. In one swift motion she jumped to her feet, poised for a fight.

Keith put his hands up in surrender. "Whoa. It's okay. It's just me."

She dropped her hands but kept a solid defensive stance. "I didn't hear you come in," she said between deep breaths.

"Yeah. Sorry. You seemed in the zone. Didn't want to interrupt that." Yeah. Sure. She'd buy that. It certainly sounded better than "I was ogling you for a minute. Hope you don't mind." Keith blinked hard to try and clear his head. He *had* to get his act together.

Torie walked over and grabbed the long-sleeved T-shirt off the hay bale. She put it on then wiped her brow with the sleeve. "Sorry. I was out for a run and found this place." Hands on her hips, she looked around. Her breathing had slowed a bit. "It's pretty great. I couldn't resist."

"No worries. It's yours to use while you're here."

"Thanks."

"Don't let me cut short your workout either."

Back out the door and leave her alone, Scott. It's better for both of you.

"I can leave..." He pointed a thumb over his shoulder

towards the door. "Or join you, if you don't mind having a workout partner." And… there went the brilliant idea of leaving. Searching her eyes for a response, he tried to ignore the *please say stay, please say stay* that chanted along with his heartbeat.

Her eyes had been guarded when he first came in. They softened as she said, "You can stay. That's fine. I actually could use a spotter on the heavier weights."

He nodded and moved inside the barn, closing the door behind him. "Sounds good. Where do you want to start?"

Without hesitating she turned towards the side wall and said, "Squat rack."

He waved her forward. "After you."

They moved around together in quiet, the only noise being the music floating from her iPod again. Keith had put together this personal gym for the times he was home, not only to stay in shape for work but also as a respite from the world. In here, the world outside melted away, along with stress and any other crap he carried from his time overseas. Right now his mind could only focus on the woman in front of him who continued to rack more weight on the bar.

"You sure you can handle that?" he asked.

Torie stopped, gave him a hardcore stare, and added on twenty more pounds. She moved under the bar, adjusting it just right along her shoulders and said, "This is just a warm-up, Captain America. Let's see if you can keep up."

He laughed and stepped behind her to spot her. They

took turns on the squat rack then moved to push press and some core work. Torie's presence was calming. They didn't talk, just moved through a workout. Keith sensed a shift in Torie. She was relaxing, leaving behind whatever was bothering her just as he did when he was in here. Curiosity burned in his gut, though, at what it was exactly she needed to leave behind.

"You wanna end with a run?" Torie's voice pulled him from his thoughts.

He hid his surprise at how she still had any energy, but, not about to be outdone by a woman said, "Sure."

They moved in sync as they put weights and equipment away. "Rescue Me" by Fontella Bass came through the iPod.

"You like the oldies, huh?" he teased.

She smiled. A tender smile that reached her eyes. "Yeah. My gram listened to them all the time. It's music that brings back happy memories."

He had a sense she didn't have many of those.

Her eyes glimmered and she said, "You dance, Captain America?"

"Maybe," he teased.

She grabbed his hand and led him to the center of the workout area. "Come on. I'll show you some old-school moves."

"Whoa!" He tried to pull back a bit but she tugged on him more. "You mean now?"

"Of course I mean now." She put a hand on her hip and

looked him up and down. "Unless you're chicken."

Her look caused a shiver through him. A chicken was the last thing he was at that moment.

"Come on!" She grabbed his hand again. She held it tight as she moved left then right then back. "Watch my feet. It's basically a triangle, but we do the opposite of one another." She kept stepping as he followed her movements. He'd been country dancing since he was in diapers so he caught on pretty fast. Their steps synced with the beat of the music. Moving with him in perfect time, she threw her head back and laughed.

"You *can* dance!" The look on her face was not unlike when she discovered twinkle lights the night before. He soaked it in like a man in a desert, her joy being the water he so desperately craved.

He pulled her to him, switching their steps so he led as he twirled her around the room. She laughed and rested her forehead on his chest.

The music stopped. Keith slowed them down until they stood in the center of the room again, still holding one another. Torie smiled up at him, and damn it if that didn't make him want to puff out his chest and announce to the world that he'd been the one to make her eyes shine.

A shot rang out from outside the barn and Torie jumped. In a split second she went from relaxed to so tense Keith could feel every muscle in her body go tight. She tried to push from his embrace but he held her close. He felt her heartbeat against his chest accelerate, adrenaline pulsing through her system.

"It's okay. Dad's target shooting, I'm sure."

She looked up at him. Her eyes were guarded again. He'd lost her.

She nodded and stepped away from him. She walked over to her iPod and clipped it back on her pants.

"I'm sorry. I should've told you. We should have warned you so you wouldn't be scared."

She turned to him. "I'm a cop, Keith. I'm not afraid of a gunshot."

He nodded, accepting her answer. For now. But she was lying. Yes, she was a cop, and quite fearless on many fronts. But she was spooked. And he wanted to know why.

Now wasn't the time to ask though. There was that tricky trust issue again. She needed to feel safe with him. Safe to share whatever it was she was worried about. Or hiding from.

"You still up for a run?" he asked.

"Absolutely."

* * *

Torie's footfalls were in sync with Keith's. Although taller than her and most likely faster, he stayed by her as they ran.

She mentally berated herself for wigging out back at the barn. Whenever she was with Keith though, she relaxed. Actually enjoyed herself. And not the kind of enjoyment she got from going out dancing and escaping for a while. Being with Keith was the most natural thing she'd ever experienced. There was no pretense, no expectations. She could just…be. It was weird. Men always wanted something from her. He'd asked for nothing. He actually seemed more interested in what she wanted or what made her happy. Huh. That was definitely a new one.

They approached a hill and she sped up, pushed and pushed until she reached the top. Her legs and lungs burned but that only propelled her forward. She stopped and looked down to the small meadow below where Dane and Aimee's cabin stood. Keith had stopped next to her, his hands on his hips, chest heaving as he caught his breath. She'd seen his chest when he took off his shirt during their workout. A USMC tattoo covered the skin over his heart. She'd been right. He was definitely romance novel cover material. And then some. Glory, the man was a sight to behold.

"You okay?"

His question brought her from her thoughts. It was a good thing too. She was staring and would probably start drooling soon. Not good.

"Yeah. Why?" She answered between deep gulps of air. "Are you struggling, Dough Boy?" She could see her breath in the cool air.

He laughed and shook his head but then got serious again. "I don't know. You were running like something was chasing you. You push yourself pretty hard."

The words tumbled out before she could stop them.

"When I push myself hard, there's no room for what chases me."

Instead of asking anything further he nodded and said, "I understand."

He looked her in the eye. He *did* understand. No one ever had before. She could only imagine the demons he ran from. Maybe, just maybe, she could trust him with hers.

"Come on." He took her hand and led her down the hill to the cabin. "I'll walk you home."

7

"SO. WHAT DO you ranch working cowboy types do for fun around here? Besides visit bookstores and work out in the barn?" Torie teased as they headed down the hill. Her hand was still tucked neatly inside of Keith's.

He laughed. "Ranch working cowboy types, huh? A city girl like you can't wrap your head around that, can ya?"

"I'm not much of a city girl, actually."

He turned to look at her as they walked. Her head was down, watching where she stepped, so he couldn't read her eyes, but her tone was soft.

She continued. "I grew up in Wyoming. I work in San Diego, but I prefer the country."

He proceeded with caution but wanted to know more. "What brought you to San Diego?"

he didn't answer right away, just continued to walk

beside him. When they reached the porch of the cabin, she pulled him with her to the side-by-side rocking chairs and they sat down.

"After my mom died, I went to live with my gram. I told her I wanted to be a cop and she encouraged me to follow my dreams."

Her rocking chair squeaked and she toyed with her fingers as she talked. She'd done that after dinner at his parents' house when they'd discussed getting a Christmas tree. A nervous gesture when vulnerable perhaps? Keith searched her eyes. A little sad, but not as lonely as usual.

"What made you want to be a cop?"

Her back stiffened a bit at that question. Interesting. He'd always been good at reading people. Something in Torie's past haunted her, he had no doubt. Finding out what without having her shut down on him was going to be the tricky part.

He thought she might not answer when she said, "I wanted to help people. People who aren't always able to help themselves."

Her eyes clouded over for sure with that. Not wanting to push her anymore, Keith rocked his chair and said, "I understand. When I joined the Marines, I wanted to help people. Serve my country."

She smiled, her body relaxing a bit at the attention being brought back his direction.

They rocked in quiet. Birds chirped overhead and the breeze whispered through the pines. It was warm for a December day. Well, warm to him. It was probably fifty-five out. Cold to some, but perfect in his book. Snow was on its way though. He hoped for Torie it would bring a magical white Christmas.

Keith laid his head back and closed his eyes. The sound of Torie's rocking chair synced with his, a symphony of calm. His world had tilted ever since this woman entered his life, and yet her presence brought something he hadn't had in years. Peace.

He struggled to wrap his head around it. Just knowing she sat beside him taking in the beauty of their surroundings, brought him comfort. In truth, he hardly knew Torie. And yet, he did know her. Was connected to her in a way he'd never been with anyone else, both terrifying and thrilling him at the same time.

"It's nice you're so close to your family."

Her voice brought him from his thoughts. He opened his eyes again and looked at her. Her head rested against the back of the chair, eyes closed as she spoke.

"Yes. They're caring, but not nosy. Well, my mom is sometimes."

They laughed. Torie blushed. Apparently his mom's matchmaking skills weren't as subtle as Keith hoped.

"Mom always means well. Family is important to me."

"You're lucky."

"Yeah, I guess I am."

* * *

Keith smiled but he sounded almost...sad. Intrigued, Torie waited for him to say more, but he didn't. He was a man of few words, that was for sure. And she didn't mind it. Not one bit. That chattier the man, the more they wanted her to chat.

She was usually guarded around men, not wanting to give too much of herself away. But with Keith, things were different. He was different. He didn't have to say much. Just his being there felt right.

She had wondered why, for a man who valued family so highly, Keith wasn't married with a family of his own by now. Not to mention the fact he was Greek god personified. He was a few years older than Dane, which would put him in his early thirties. The comment from the woman in the bookstore came to mind. Women were interested in him. He just wasn't reciprocating the feeling. So why so much attention on her?

She snuck a peek at him out of the corner of her eye. His military haircut blended with the scruff he'd let grow over the past few days. She smiled. A soldier's version of "letting your hair down" a bit. His eyes were focused on the trees beyond but she knew the deep blue like her own reflection. You didn't stare into eyes like that and not have them become a permanent part of your memory.

His mouth was turned down in a slight frown. Yep. Talking about family had hit a nerve. She just couldn't figure out what nerve that might be. Colt and Ellie were loving, giving parents. Dane was the kind of brother she'd give her right arm for. Her family had practically written the book on dysfunction. She couldn't fathom what could possibly bother Keith about his.

"So, you asked what we cowboy types do for fun around

here." He turned his head and smiled at her, all evidence of any previous angst was gone.

"Yes, I did."

"Well, I'm meeting some friends for dinner tonight and dancing. You're welcome to join us. You know, if you can keep up. It's country dancing. Not this '60s stuff you seem so keen on."

The glimmer in his eye paired with his teasing turned her insides to goo. The memory of him holding her close in the barn not long ago, twirling her around and making her forget her troubles, had her heart skipping a beat as well.

She sat up straight in her chair and leaned towards him. "Is that some sort of challenge, Captain America?"

He met her halfway. "Maybe it is."

Oh, this was gonna be fun. "You're on."

He laughed. A from the gut, all male sound that made her insides tingle. "I'll pick you up at six, so be ready." He stood and stepped off the porch. "Don't forget your best dancing boots, Dragonfly." With that, he winked and took off jogging through the trees.

* * *

Dragonfly? Why had he called her Dragonfly? Torie checked herself in the mirror for about the tenth time, grateful she'd brought cute jeans and her favorite country top. It was a deep green with a brown design throughout and scattered with bling. She'd also thrown in her higher-heeled cowgirl boots and thanked the Lord above she could finally wear them and not tower over every man in the room. At least not the man she'd be with. Bonus. Big bonus.

Keith *was* a big bonus. She'd imagined her few weeks off to be slow. Full of reading and hikes. Lots of time alone. And she was fine with that. Was used to it. She was even prepared for a Christmas all by herself. Well, sort of prepared. Loneliness was a buzzing fly, definitely unwelcomed, and usually crept in at the most inconvenient times.

But she didn't have to be lonely tonight. She did love to go out dancing, and it had been a while since she'd done so with someone as appealing as Keith. And he could dance. Another bonus. This was shaping up to be a much better day than she'd imagined.

The voice mail from that morning played in her head, plummeting her good feelings. No. She wouldn't think about that now. Couldn't. There was no way he'd find her all the way up north in a remote area tucked away. Besides, she'd have Keith with her too. She was safe with Keith.

A knock on the door brought her from her thoughts. She checked herself in the mirror one last time, grabbed her coat and purse, and answered the door. Keith stood on the porch, a black cowboy hat accenting his blue eyes and a grin that spelled trouble with a capital T. With jeans that fit him just right, a black button-down shirt, and shiny boots to complete the package, he was exactly the kind of trouble worth diving into.

She pulled the door closed behind her and said, "You look great."

"You too. You ready?"

"For your dance challenge? Absolutely."

He laughed again, the one that made her tummy do flips. Oh yeah. He was her kind of trouble.

They climbed into his truck as she asked, "So, where exactly are we going?"

Keith guided the truck down the dirt road away from the cabin and towards the entrance to the 4S Ranch. "We're meeting my friend, Tony, and his wife, Rae, at The Barn."

"The Barn?" Torie raised her eyebrows.

"Yep. You heard me right. A couple moved into town about three years ago from Texas and turned a barn into a country western tavern. Great food and some good tunes for dancing.'" He winked.

The thought ran through Torie's mind once more as to how this man hadn't been snagged and claimed by a woman yet, but she swatted it away. She didn't like the thought of Keith with anyone else and if he had been claimed at any point, it wasn't any of her business. He was here now. With her. That was all that mattered.

They drove into town, the music from the radio filling the car. Torie recognized the bookstore as they passed and a small coffee shop she made note to get back to and try one day. They turned down a side road and sure enough, off the beaten path stood a huge barn with neon lights above the door welcoming all to The Barn. Keith parked his truck along the side of the building and came around to open Torie's door for her. A couple came out through the front doors. The bass from the music pumped through her as she hopped out.

He took her hand and led her through the entrance. Torie

took in her surroundings. A large dance floor made up the center of the building. An upstairs balcony wrapped around the entire building and looked out over the floor. High tables were scattered about upstairs where people sat and ate while watching dancers below. Small tables flanked the dance floor while booths lined the outside walls.

"Come on. I see Tony and Rae."

Keith led her to a booth against the wall away from the dance floor. It was tough to ignore the chorus of "Hi Keiths" that came from various women as they made their way through the tables. Also difficult to miss the stares Torie received from said women since Keith was gripping her hand like a lifeline as if he swam through treacherous waters and she was the only thing keeping him from being swallowed whole.

A couple occupied one side of the booth already. The man stood and gave Keith a bear hug. He wasn't nearly as tall as Keith but he was just as broad. Torie recognized right away he was military, not just because his hair was cut similar to Keith's but from the way he carried himself as well. He had olive skin and dark eyes. His wife stood too and hugged Keith, who had to almost bend in half to embrace her tiny frame. The polar opposite of her husband, her hair was bright red and hung in waves to her shoulders. Emerald green eyes popped out amidst freckles that sprinkled along her fair skin.

"Hey, Hulk. Glad you could join us," Rae said as she patted his chest and took her seat in the booth once again.

"Hulk?" Torie looked at him and grinned. Based on the look Keith gave Rae, this was gonna be good.

"It's a nickname of sorts," Keith mumbled. "Torie, this

is Tony and Rae Ambrosi. Guys, this is Torie." Keith hung their coats on a rack near the booth and sat next to Torie, across from Rae and Tony.

"You're not getting out of the Hulk explanation, you know that, right?" Torie said as he sat down.

Tony laughed. "Oh, I like her. It's somewhat of a nickname we gave this beast in the Marine Corps."

"You two serve together?" Torie asked.

"Yes ma'am." Tony nodded.

"Hmmm, I think more Captain America, but I can see where Hulk can work too."

"Just keep going on, you two, as if I'm not here," Keith grumbled.

"We will." Torie patted his shoulder.

"So, Keith tells us you're visiting for the holidays. That's nice." Rae smiled at Torie.

"I am. My roommate, Aimee, married Keith's brother. She invited me to hang out in their cabin while they're on their honeymoon."

"That's lovely. I hear their place is beautiful."

"It is," Torie agreed. "Keith did a great job on the place."

Keith cleared his throat. "It wasn't all me."

Rae swiped a hand his direction. "Always being modest, this one."

Torie turned and looked at Keith. Pointing a thumb his direction she said, "This one? Modest? Are you sure?"

Tony laughed again. "Oh yeah, this one's a keeper for sure. She's got you pegged already, Hulk."

The waitress approached their table and Keith's relief was

palpable. Shoulder to shoulder in the booth, Torie could feel him relax at the saving grace that placing their order gave in terms of them not talking about him anymore. Not only that, but when Tony had said she was a keeper, Keith's whole body tightened. Was the thought of them being a couple so horrible to him? He'd acted otherwise so far in their time together. Fair enough. She noted his reaction and filed it under, "May not be as into you as you might think. Or want him to be." The thought turned her gut and she sat back in the booth, not as full of courage as she was moments before.

She placed her order and handed over the menu. Keith smiled at her but it wasn't like the ones he'd sent her way the past couple of days.

"Why don't you two take a spin on the dance floor before our food comes," Tony suggested.

Torie tensed, not sure dancing was what Keith wanted right now.

But he stood and held out his hand. "I guess now is as good a time as any to see how well you do in *my* kind of barn."

She reached out her hand to his. "Challenge accepted, Captain."

8

KEITH REACHED THE dance floor and spun Torie into his arms. Man, he loved how she fit perfect right against him. She'd sensed his agitation at Tony saying she was a keeper. As if Torie would ever be his to keep. He'd learned the hard way that what he did with his life wasn't meant to burden someone else. Sure, Tony and Rae made it work, but they were rare. Not everyone was cut out for military life. Keith accepted that and vowed to never ask another woman to bear that load with him again.

He swept them across the dance floor as Florida Georgia Line sang about wanting to roll the windows down and cruise.

"You okay?" Torie looked up at him, her body relaxed in his arms, following his steps without effort. She really was a good dancer. And he sensed how much she trusted him. All the more reason he needed to stop being a jerk and have a nice evening with her. Hell, he invited her here. Now he was getting wrapped up in his past instead of focusing on the beautiful woman in his arms.

"Yeah. Sorry. Just got distracted for a bit there."

"You wanna talk about it?"

The sincerity in her eyes melted his heart. It had been a long time since a woman was willing to listen to him. Most only wanted something from him—a ring on their hand and a claim to him in some way. It was beyond annoying. Even now he could feel the stares of the women around them. Surely they were wondering who this bombshell was in his arms and how she managed to get there. Hell. He was wondering that very thing himself.

Torie was different. Special. Self-sufficient and capable. So far, she'd asked nothing of him. She didn't need him, and that made him want her even more.

"Nah. It's nothing. I'm sorry. I invited you out and now I'm afraid I'm a dud of a date." He smiled down at her and shifted their movements as the song changed.

"Are we on a date, Captain?" Her eyes twinkled with her teasing.

"You keep calling me that and people are gonna think that's my rank. Which it isn't, by the way."

"Oh really? Well, I figure you'd rather be called Captain than Hulk."

He winced. "You have a point there."

She laughed. "Speaking of nicknames. You called me Dragonfly earlier. I'll admit, you've got me curious. I mean, we know why I call you Captain America, but Dragonfly? I'm lost."

"I actually *don't* know exactly why you call me Captain America, but you're right, I like it better than Hulk as nicknames go. I don't like nicknames at all, but for you I'll make an exception." He winked.

"You're stalling."

"Oh. Right. Dragonfly." He shrugged. "I don't know. It just seemed to fit."

"You saw fit to call me a bug?"

He laughed and pulled her closer to him. "No. Not at all. I've always thought of dragonflies as beautiful. They're a mix of delicacy and strength, just like you."

She stiffened in his arms and stopped moving her feet, causing him to do the same. He maneuvered them to the edge of the dance floor so they wouldn't get bumped. "I'm sorry. Did I upset you?"

She blinked and shook her head. "No. No. I'm sorry." She relaxed again. "Let's keep dancing."

He guided them back into the flow of couples. Unsure if what he said was good or bad, he searched her eyes. He could find her secrets there if he just kept looking.

She smiled up at him. Her eyes were soft. That was a good sign. "Thank you."

"For?"

"For saying that. It was...nice."

She laid her head on his chest and sank into him, moving with him again without effort. At that moment, everything and everyone else in the room faded away. It was a world with him and Torie alone. He liked that world. And he wanted it. More than he'd ever wanted anything before in his life.

* * *

Torie melted into Keith. The man could move, she'd say that about him. Relaxed against him, she followed his lead around the dance floor, soaking him in. It was divine to dance with a man she could actually look up to. One who didn't make her feel huge. His arms enveloped her, her faced tucked into his neck. He smelled of leather and pine. All male. So yummy.

He hadn't explained his discomfort back at the table, but things were fine now. That was good enough for her. The moment was better than any she'd had in a mighty long time.

Her knees had all but turned to jelly when he explained why he called her Dragonfly. Her strength usually turned men away. It intimidated them. And she'd certainly never been considered delicate. Feminine, maybe, but somehow the tough side of her always overpowered the rest. Men didn't seem to want to stick around long enough to get to know her delicate side. Keith saw it without even trying.

Even today while they'd worked out, he acted impressed by her abilities but still made her feel like...well, a girl. Living in a man's world, she sometimes lost that side of her. Wanting to be treated equally, she wore a tough exterior at work, but in truth, it got exhausting. With Keith, she could let her hair down and just be.

"You still haven't told me why you call me Captain America."

She smiled. "Come on. You don't know you've got that smoldering, good guy soldier-boy thing going on?"

He chuckled in her ear. She shivered. In a good way.

"Smoldering, huh?" His voice dipped low, causing her tummy to drop as well. "I do recall now you saying something like that the morning I brought you breakfast."

Uh-oh. Hadn't thought through that word before it left her mouth. She shrugged but didn't answer. If she wasn't careful she'd follow her gut and kiss him right there on the dance floor. Without mistletoe. In front of the all the drooling women nearby. Hmmm, that actually sounded rather appealing on a lot of levels, now that she thought about it.

His chest moved again with a laugh. "Now you're thinking so hard I can see your mind spinning."

"Can you tell what I'm thinking?"

He looked into her eyes. The steel blue went from soft to sultry. She swallowed. Hard. Apparently she wasn't the only one thinking of hot kisses, even if half the town was watching.

The song ended and the DJ's voice boomed through the room. Torie blinked and the moment was gone. Keith took her hand and guided them back to their table. The food had arrived, sprawled out in front of Tony and Rae.

"We waited for you like one pig waits for another," Tony said with a mouthful of French fry.

Rae smacked his arm. "Mind your manners. Don't talk with your mouth full."

She looked at Keith and Torie as they took their seats in the booth. "He's right though. We're starving. You two looked like you were enjoying yourselves so we dove in without ya."

"No worries." Torie placed her napkin in her lap and took a long swig of water. The dancing, among other things, had certainly turned up her body heat.

"You know what you're doing out there, Torie," Rae said. It was a compliment.

"I've always loved to dance. My gram taught me some moves as well when I lived with her. Showed a few of those to Keith here today." She smiled at Keith. Was he blushing?

"That's nice," Rae continued, oblivious to Keith's discomfort. Tony noticed it though, and chuckled.

"Needed some dance lessons, did ya, Hulk?" Tony teased.

Keith leaned back in the booth and eyed his friend. He smirked. "I can dance circles around your butt any day, soldier, and you know it. You're just jealous."

Tony laughed out loud.

"Oh, you two." Rae smiled. "Settle down. You both know that *I'm* the best dancer of the group, so back yourselves down."

The two men frowned and looked at Rae. Torie smiled. Oh, she liked this woman.

Rae continued. "And from what I've seen of Torie here, I've got some new competition." She winked. "After we eat and they get to the line dancing part of the evening, we women will show you boys how it's done."

She raised her glass and Torie toasted her. Oh yeah. Rae was her kind of people.

Both men shook their heads and dove into their meals. Torie liked the camaraderie between the three of them. It was obvious they were close.

"So, how long have you two been married?" Torie asked.

Rae's eyes lit up as Torie expected. "Three years."

Tony leaned over and kissed his wife's cheek. "I'd be lost without this one, that's for sure."

Keith avoiding eye contact with any of them wasn't lost on Torie. She was a cop. She could read people, situations. He was uncomfortable—again.

"How did you two meet?

"Through a group at church, actually," Rae answered. Tony happily munched his food while his wife talked. Keith ate as well, but wasn't as relaxed as when they sat down.

"I'm a counselor that runs a group through our church. I work mainly with people who struggle with PTSD."

Torie nodded and took a sip of her water. Now it was her turn to be uncomfortable. She'd read about PTSD and even considered she might have it herself with all she'd been through, but talking about it wasn't gonna happen. That was for sure.

"So what do you do for a living, Torie?" Rae stole a fry from Tony's plate. He swatted her hand playfully.

"I'm a cop."

Tony's eyebrows lifted. "Really? Ow!" He rubbed his leg and glared at Rae.

Torie laughed. "It's okay. I get that reaction a lot."

Tony eyed his wife cautiously. "You just don't..."

"Look the type. I know." Torie munched on a celery stick from the hot wings basket.

"Sorry." Rae gave her husband the evil eye. He shrugged and looked legitimately confused.

Keith laughed.

"What?" Torie asked, glad he joined the conversation.

"Nothin. I just had the same thought as well that first day you pulled up in your rusty old truck."

Torie's jaw dropped. "How dare you! My truck is not rusty."

Keith pointed at her. "But you admit that it's old."

She closed her mouth and frowned. "I admit no such thing. And you've never said a word about that day."

He shrugged. "We were focused on Dane and Aimee. But I agree with Tony. Your first impression isn't cop."

Tony looked at Rae as if to say, *"See? I'm not the only one."*

"So what *was* your first impression of me?"

Keith's jaw twitched and he looked away. He had to think

about his answer, did he? Well, she wouldn't fess up to him either what *her* first impression of *him* was. She'd gotten out of her truck and walked over to the corral where he was training a new horse. He was the most beautiful man she'd ever seen. And the way he guided the large animal beneath him with grace and patience was a sight to behold. He'd blown her away. Of course, then he'd gone toe to toe with her about how to handle Aimee's situation. That ruffled her feathers, but only because her attraction to the man was off the charts. And most men didn't cross her. They just…didn't.

"Oh, would you idiotic men just say what you're thinking." Rae jumped in. She looked straight at Torie. "You must know this, girlfriend. You could be a supermodel. You really don't scream cop, which makes me like you all the more. A kick-butt woman inside that exterior? I can stand up and applaud that."

Torie smiled at the woman across from her. Not unlike Aimee, Rae had the fire of a redhead, for sure. And that was the first time that description of herself didn't bother her. Most women were intimidated by her. Rae honestly saw her as an equal. It was refreshing, to say the least.

"Ok. I'm done with you two men," Rae went on. She pushed on Tony's arm. "Let me out of this booth. They're playing my favorite song and it's line dancing time. Come on, Torie." She waved at Torie to join her.

Torie smiled and nudged Keith as well. He moved and gave her his hand to help her out of the booth. His touch brought back their near kiss on the dance floor and her cheeks flushed with heat. She mustered a weak, "Thanks" then followed Rae through the tables to the dance floor.

* * *

Keith and Tony sat in the booth and watched the girls dance as they slid and scooted along the floor. Rae was right. She could out-dance all of them. Although Torie was a super-close second and the woman he couldn't peel his eyes from.

"You've got it bad, man." Tony shoved the last bite of his burger into his mouth.

Keith shook his head. "Shut up."

Tony grinned. "You know I'm right. You can't take your eyes off her and you're all fussy under the collar. I've never seen you this way. Not even with…"

"Don't." Keith put a hand up to stop his friend. "I don't want to talk about her tonight."

Tony nodded. "Fair enough. Sorry." He wadded up his napkin and tossed it on his empty plate. "I'm just sayin'. It might be time for you to venture out again. I'm not saying you have to marry anyone. Just go on a few dates. Get out there again."

Keith shook his head. "No. That's pointless."

"Look, man. I know you've got it in your head somehow that your life isn't cut out for marriage, but look at me and Rae. You can make it work."

Keith turned his attention back to Torie. She threw her head back and laughed at something Rae said then shook her hips to the music. Tony was right. He had it bad. She had him turned upside down and sideways.

"I love my wife more than life itself, but I'm not blind. Torie is beautiful. And she brings something out in you I haven't seen in a really long time."

Keith looked at his friend. "Oh yeah? What's that?"

"A smile, idiot. She makes you happy. And you've got yourself stuck in some stupid mental rut that says you don't deserve to be happy. But you're wrong."

Keith shook his head again. Maybe Tony was right. Maybe he was letting the past control his future. He still had doubts. "But I barely know her." The words sounded lame, even to him.

"Then get to know her. You've gotta pray about letting this go, man. The crap you hold onto. Life is messy, yes. But we aren't designed to go through it alone."

Tony leaned his elbows on the table and looked Keith in the eye. "She's special and you know it. Don't let this chance pass you by because you're too stubborn to grab on while you can."

Keith took a deep breath. Tony was right. He had to let go of the past and move forward. He'd like to do that with Torie. See where their paths might lead.

He smiled. "Thanks."

Tony leaned back again in the booth. "I'm happy to kick

you in the butt anytime."

Keith laughed and looked again to the dance floor. His smile faded, however, and his gut churned. The song had changed and couples were forming. A tall man in a dark brown cowboy hat had his arms around Torie. Keith couldn't see the man's face, but the fire that ran through his blood told him exactly who it was. All that Tony had just said flew out of Keith's head. The past smacked into him like a punch to the jaw and he only saw red.

9

THE SONG ENDED and Torie turned to follow Rae back to their table. She couldn't remember the last time she'd had this much fun out for an evening country dancing. As she reached the edge of the dance floor a firm hand gripped hers and spun her around. A man about her height in a brown cowboy hat pulled her close and said, "Can I have the honor of this next dance, my lady?"

The next song began and he moved them to the center of the dance floor in a few steps and a spin.

"Doesn't look like I have much of choice now, does it?"

He smiled. It wasn't unfriendly but something inside Torie prickled.

"Oh, you always have a choice, darlin'. I'm just asking for one little dance."

Torie moved along with him to the music but stayed cautious. She'd seen this guy's type before. Danced with too many of them. They were usually harmless but she kept her ears perked and eyes wide open just in case.

"You must be new in town. Pretty thing like you I would've noticed for sure by now."

"I'm visiting." The less this creep knew about her the better.

"That's too bad. Place like this could sure use a stunner like you."

Torie looked around. "I don't know. Looks like there are some lovely ladies here tonight. I'm sure you could take your pick."

His hand moved dangerously low down Torie's back as he said, "But you're the one I'm choosin' tonight, darlin'."

Torie moved his hand up to her back where it belonged. "Let's dance for now. No picking and choosing necessary."

"But I'm just the man you need, gorgeous. You just don't know it yet."

His hand slid down again, this time cupping her backside and pulling her closer to him.

All right. She'd had enough of this yahoo. Moving her hand again to grab his and twist him into a hold that would have him screaming Uncle, she stopped when she heard, "Let her go, Clint."

Keith's voice was low but there was no mistaking the venom behind it. Torie turned to see him standing behind her, his eyes intense and his stance ready for a fight. Good Lord, now she understood what Aimee meant about him being imposing. Anyone in their right mind would be a fool to go up against him. Unfortunately, her dance partner seemed just idiotic enough to try. Keith had at least five inches on this guy and although Clint wasn't scrawny, he was no match for Keith's bulk.

"Don't get your panties all in a ruffle, Keith. I'm just dancing with the lady."

Keith didn't move. Didn't even blink. "You and I both know you were doing more than dancing. I'm gonna ask one more time, nicely, and if you don't listen, I'll handle you outside. Get your hands off her."

For a brief moment Torie thought Clint might taunt Keith some more. Instead, he released her and put his hands up in surrender. "Fine. Whatever. Like always, you sure know how to ruin a guy's evening."

Keith took Torie's hand and gently guided her beside him. "Go home to your wife, Clint."

That knocked Clint's cocky attitude down a few notches. He scowled at Keith then turned and walked away.

Up against Keith's side, Torie could feel his adrenaline pumping. He was using every ounce of strength he had to control himself. She could only imagine what this man was like if his anger was unleashed.

He looked down at her, his eyes still intense but softening for her. "Are you okay?"

"Yeah. I'm fine. I was about to put him in a choke hold when you came along."

One corner of his mouth turned up slightly, but his body language still said he was a long ways from calming down.

"I like her more and more each minute, Hulk." Tony said. He and Rae were standing behind them. Torie didn't even realize it until now. They literally had Keith's back.

Keith still stared at her. "Are you sure you're okay? I didn't mean to frighten you."

Frighten her? Because he was angry? She stared back at him and then understood. "No. I could never be afraid of you." She cupped his cheek in her hand and placed a tender kiss on his lips. When she pulled back, Keith looked surprised, but then gave her slight smile. One only she could see.

"Let's get out of here." His voice was a whisper.

She nodded.

He turned and led them off the dance floor, Tony and Rae following behind.

* * *

They said good night to Tony and Rae, with Rae and Torie making plans to meet for coffee soon, then Keith opened Torie's door for her and tucked her in his truck. He took his time getting around to his door, breathing in and out deeply as he walked. He was still coming down from the scene with Clint.

He'd seen red when Clint first snagged Torie for a dance, but his entire body raged when Clint started getting fresh with her. Hulk apparently was an appropriate nickname. He was surprised he didn't become some massive monster of anger and rage. He'd sure felt that way inside. In his entire life he'd never had to control himself the way he did tonight. He wasn't jealous. Torie would never go for a guy like Clint. Protective? Hell, yes. Torie might be able to take care of herself, but that was beside the point. Everything in him wanted to wrap her up in his arms and tell the world she was his. Keith shook his head as he climbed in the truck. He was falling for her and falling hard.

He started the engine and guided the vehicle onto the main road. Torie didn't say anything, just sat quietly on her side of the front seat.

He rubbed his mouth with one hand, the other on the steering wheel. His hand shook a bit still. He'd need another full-on workout tonight when he got home to deal with this crap. The night had been going well. Really well. Torie was having fun. He was even having fun. Like Tony said. He was smiling again. And damn it, it felt good. Then like a ton of bricks, Clint dropped in. Of all the friggin' bad luck. Right when he was considering moving forward, his past crashed in and derailed him. He shook his head and took a deep breath.

"Are you okay?"

Torie's voice brought him from his thoughts.

He managed a nod. She'd known exactly what he meant

when he asked if she was frightened. Of course she wasn't scared of Clint. She could kick his butt from here to Sunday. Keith was concerned his anger would make her afraid of *him*. Make her think of her dad. Whatever the bastard had done to her Keith could only imagine, and that imagination had him ready and willing to wring the man's neck. When she'd reached up and kissed him, his anger stilled and he only saw her. She trusted him. *Trust*. He missed that.

"You do know I could've handled myself with that guy."

Keith nodded. He still didn't trust his voice yet, let alone the words that might come out of his mouth

"Okay. No talking. That's fair." She scooted closer and put her head on his shoulder. "Just so you know, that's the first time a man has ever come to rescue me. Don't tell anyone, but I kinda liked it."

He could feel her smile against his arm. He peeked down at her, the lights from the dash casting a glow over her face. His very own angel in blue jeans. Could she ever truly be his though? His heart ached to say yes, but the scene with Clint reminded his brain he should say no.

She looked up at him. The glimmer from those hazel eyes took any doubts in the world he'd ever had and melted them like butter. Her eyes were far from lonely at the moment and that made him happy. Huh. Tony's words came to mind again. He was happy when he was with Torie.

He relaxed a bit and took her hand in his. He'd never met a woman like her. She didn't push. Didn't make him talk. Just accepted him as is. His truck bounced along the dirt road that led to Dane and Aimee's place. Alison Krauss's voice floated through the cab of his truck singing about two hearts speaking to one another, no words necessary. Boy, didn't that hit home. This woman leaning on him didn't have to say a word and yet could read his every thought, every feeling. He sensed the same with her.

He'd told Tony he didn't know Torie, but it wasn't true. This woman was made for him. His gut believed that as much as he believed the sun would rise and set every day. He just didn't have a single damn idea what to do about it.

* * *

Keith didn't say a word the entire trip back to the cabin. Torie understood. That kind of adrenaline rush took time to come down from. And she was no fool. Clint wasn't some random jerk at a dance club. He and Keith knew each other. And most definitely not in a good way. But pushing Keith for answers would only make him clam up. He kept things close to the vest. She understood that as well.

They pulled up to Dane and Aimee's place and Keith came around to open her door. Taking her hand, he led her to the front porch. When they reached the front door he pulled her to him, hugging her close. She buried her face in his neck and accepted his embrace.

"I'm sorry about tonight." His voice rumbled his chest

against hers.

"I'm not. It was fun."

He chuckled. "Your idea of fun is unusual."

She pulled back a bit and looked up at him. "It was fun. I'm not willing to let five minutes with one creep ruin the rest of my evening, and you shouldn't be either."

He nodded, his hat bobbing up and down with the movement.

Torie leaned into him, bringing her lips to his. Their kiss started out soft and tender but moved to hot and heavy in a hurry. Her arms wrapped around his waist under his coat, his hands weaving pure magic through her hair. It could've lasted five minutes or an hour, Torie had no clue, nor did she care. She'd do this all night. Keith's response to her said he was more than willing to oblige.

He held her face in his hands and pulled back, both of them catching their breath. Placing his forehead to hers he said, "I think it's time for me to go."

"You sure, Captain? You okay with just a kiss?" Most men weren't. Torie knew that all too well.

He laughed and kissed her again, a soft sweet kiss lasting only a moment. "Honestly? No. But for now, the answer is yes ma'am." He tilted her head up and looked her in the eye. "I fear you haven't known men in your life to have self-control. I figure it's about time you see what that looks like."

She took his hands in hers and shook her head. "Just when I think I have you figured out, Captain, you throw me a curve ball."

He gave her a full-on dimple-filled smile that made her knees week. As if they weren't already rubbery from his kiss.

"Good. I like to keep you guessing."

"Are we gonna keep guessing about this?" She pointed a finger between them. "What this is about, you and me? Where it's going?"

His smile wavered and he pulled her to him again, tucked her into his coat. "Let's take it one day at a time. Can we do that?"

She nodded, her cheek against his warm chest. Yeah, she could do that. Unlike any man in her life before, Keith wanted to go slow. A foreign concept to her, yes, but one she was more than willing to accept if it meant having Keith in her life. For how long, she didn't know. But she'd take now. She breathed in deep, the scent of Keith filling her senses. Yeah. Now was good.

Keith opened the door for her and got her safely inside. He turned at the threshold and gave her a soft kiss. "You ever go horseback riding?"

The question caught her off guard. "Um, no, actually. I grew up around ranches, and horses were everywhere but...no, I don't ride."

"Well, you will tomorrow. Be ready at nine a.m. sharp." He winked and placed a soft kiss on her lips. "Good night, Dragonfly."

And with that he was gone.

* * *

Torie washed her face and got ready for bed. The clock said it was time to sleep but her body sure didn't agree. Or her mind. She stared at the cushy, welcoming bed in the guest room and shook her head. Nope. As inviting as it was, there was no way she was ready for sleep. Not after the night she'd just had.

She padded downstairs, puffy pink socks covering her feet. She got a fire going in the fireplace and curled up under a blanket on the sofa. There really wasn't anything better in life than pajama pants, a favorite T-shirt, and fuzzy socks. The little things in life. Gram taught her to appreciate those, for sure.

The scene between Keith and Clint played over and over again in her mind. Keith's body language had rage written all over it, and not from the simple act of Clint getting fresh with her. It was a deep-seated anger from a history together. What kind of history, she had no clue. Which only reminded her how much she didn't know about Keith.

But although she didn't know *about* him, she did know *him*. The kind of man he was. And that was what mattered. His past didn't matter to her. But would hers matter to him? Her heart sank. Keith was a man of honor. He proved that tonight on her doorstep.

She'd had boyfriends before, and yes, a few she'd gone

too far with. Her age-old nemesis of shame washed over her. She'd never gotten *too* serious with a guy. Always kept things light. But she didn't want to do light with Keith. For the first time in her life, she wanted depth in a relationship. But would Keith want that with her?

A tear worked its way down her cheek and landed on her hand. She wiped it away. She looked towards the fire and sighed. Silver writing atop a purple-covered book caught her eye on the shelf under the coffee table. She reached over and picked it up, placing it in her lap.

Aimee's Bible. She recognized it from when they lived together. Aimee would sit and read it every morning while she had coffee. The pages were worn and so many parts were highlighted it looked like a rainbow exploded inside. Torie smiled. She missed her friend.

Torie went to church with Aimee when she could, when she wasn't working. And she listened to the pastor same as she had as a young girl every Sunday when she sat in a pew next to Gram. Words like love and forgiveness were waved around, phrases like washing our hearts clean. And Torie wanted to believe it. So, so much she wanted to believe it. But how could God love her, how could Jesus die for her?

She flipped through the pages and landed on the book of Psalms. Gram liked those best. "Always gives me hope, little one," she'd say to Torie. Torie read through a few chapters until her eyes were tired.

As she drifted off to sleep, she thought of how, after

living with Gram, she felt loved. Loved, yes, but never washed clean. Could God forgive her? Could Keith? She allowed dreams of sweet kisses from Keith to pull her away, afraid to know the answer.

10

TORIE WOKE WITH a kink in her neck and the blanket twisted around her legs. The fire had long gone out and there was a chill in the room. With a shiver, she unwound the blanket from her legs and burrowed down beneath it. The clock on the mantle said seven a.m. She still had plenty of time before Keith showed up.

What was she thinking? She'd never ridden a horse before. She wasn't afraid of much. Still, the thought of sitting atop an animal that large made her nervous. Her brain must have still been scrambled from their kiss last night when Keith said they were going riding, otherwise she would've listened to common sense and said a polite, "No, thank you."

Instead, she found herself mustering up the energy to drag her butt into the shower to warm up and prepare for heaven only knew what the day would bring.

Once she was showered and dressed, it was only eight o'clock so she munched on a leftover almond croissant and powered through most of the pot of coffee she'd brewed before her shower.

She was sitting at the kitchen table reading the news on her iPad when her phone rang. Aimee's goofy grin lit up the phone screen and Torie's heart filled at the sight of her friend.

"Hey, you!"

"Hey, yourself." Aimee's voice on the other end of the line sent warmth through Torie. The truest friend Torie'd ever had in the world, the woman was like a sister to her.

"You're supposed to be completely enthralled with your new husband on your honeymoon, little one. Not wasting time calling me," Torie teased, but was beyond grateful for her friend's call.

"Well, he is enthrall-worthy, I'll agree, but he's out skiing for the morning while I lounge around the cabin."

"You two crack me up. You have a perfectly gorgeous cabin in the mountains to *live in* and you go to Colorado to ski and hang out *in a cabin* for your honeymoon. Why aren't you lying on a beach in Tahiti or something soaking up the sun?"

"Honey, with my skin, the less sun, the better."

"Aimee, you grew up in San Diego. Surfing."

"Yeah, yeah. I know. That's different."

Torie had no clue how that was different but let Aimee continue. The way Aimee viewed life, her "quirks" as she called them, was one of the things Torie loved most about her.

"And honey, if you had a man like Dane to hole up with in the cold, you'd think Christmas in Colorado too."

Torie laughed. Aimee was winking at her from a few states away, she was sure of it.

"How are things going there?"

"Great." It sounded lame as soon as she said it. Aimee was sure to pounce. Three, two, one…

"Hmmm, that sounds fishy. Your 'great' sounds not great at all. Spill…"

It wasn't the first time in their friendship Torie thought of spilling everything to Aimee. Maybe she should. She'd let Keith know more about her than anyone else. And Torie trusted Aimee. Which was saying a lot. But now was not the time. Not over the phone and certainly not while Aimee was on her honeymoon and living in marital bliss.

She decided to shelve that conversation for when Aimee got back. "Honestly, things are great. Colt and Ellie have had me over for dinner and Keith has been…nice."

"Whoa, whoa. Back that truck up, sister. There is so much more than 'nice' going on in your voice right now."

Torie giggled.

"And you don't giggle. Tell me, tell me, tell me. I want to know everything."

Shuffling noises came through the phone as Aimee said, "Hold on. I'm getting a blanket and my tea. Gotta get comfy for this one."

Oh man, did Torie miss her friend.

"Ok. I'm settled now. Go. And leave nothing out."

Torie poured herself another cup of coffee and proceeded to fill Aimee in on the past few days. She didn't leave anything out. She told her friend everything, from picking out a Christmas tree, to Keith facing down Clint the night before, down to the toe-curling kiss on Aimee's own front porch.

"O...M...G!!" Aimee squealed. "I knew it. I knew it! I *so* called this. Remember? Remember the day you two first met and I said there were sparks flying between you two but you totally blew me off?"

Torie laughed. She remembered all right. She did blow Aimee off. She had no clue what to do with the pull she felt towards Keith at the time. She certainly didn't know how to explain it to Aimee.

"This is so amazing. I'm so happy for you. Oh my gosh! If you two get married we'll be like sisters. And he's so tall! That's awesome. Because, let's face it, the chances of you finding a guy taller than you were slimmer than slim and none. He really doesn't scare you though?"

Torie's mind flashed to the night before when Keith asked her if she was afraid. But that wasn't what Aimee meant. Aimee was five foot nothing. To her, Keith was a giant. And their first meeting hadn't been all warm and fuzzy either. They'd warmed up to each other over the past few months,

Keith now fiercely protective of his new sister-in-law and Aimee gushing at what a hunk he was. But Aimee was aware that people saw him as imposing.

"No. He doesn't scare me. He never could. I'm safe with him."

"Oh, sister friend. You've got it bad."

"Okay, little one. You need to calm yourself down. You are going way too far down the road here. It's been a few days and a few kisses. Don't go decorating my truck with a Just Married sign and tin cans just yet."

"Whatever." Torie imagined Aimee waving her hand around as she talked. Aimee was in constant motion. "I know you. You've never sounded this way over a guy before."

Torie couldn't deny that.

Aimee's voice softened. "And hey, you deserve a guy like Keith. And I think he needs someone like you."

"What do you mean?" Torie's sip of coffee got stuck in her throat. She coughed.

"I mean that Keith would take care of you. I know you're Miss Awesome Cop Woman and all, but even *you* need someone to lean on. And Keith has...well, he's been hurt."

"Aimee..."

"In all honesty, I don't know the whole story. Dane just said he was burned pretty badly before so he's cautious about falling for anyone. But it sounds like he's pretty comfortable with you. You're good for each other."

Torie took a deep breath and rubbed her eyes. If only

that were true. Could it be? Could she and Keith have a chance at a future together? One day at a time. That was the deal she'd made with him. That was the deal she'd stick with.

"I miss you, little one."

"I miss you too. I gotta go. Dane will be back soon. We're going sledding this afternoon." Her friend's joy was palpable through the phone line.

"I'm glad you found a co-adventurer in life, my friend. Go have fun. And tell Dane I said hi."

"I will. Love you."

"Love you too."

Torie ended the call and set her phone on the kitchen table. The only other person she'd ever said she loved was Gram. She and Aimee became roommates a couple years back via mutual friends. Where Torie was all rationale and common sense, Aimee was unicorns and rainbows. Torie was six feet tall, Aimee was almost a foot shorter. They were like the Odd Couple. But Aimee took Torie in and loved her without question. Didn't push her to talk about her past. Accepted her as she was. She invited her to church and talked about God the way Gram did. She simply lived her faith. Joy flowed from her like sunrays. Torie had no idea until they met how much she needed that in her life. Wanted it.

And she'd wanted to tell Aimee her story so many times, but every time the fear of rejection crept its way in. She couldn't stand to lose Aimee too. Doubt toyed with her mind. What if Keith turned from her too? Her heart hurt just thinking about it.

She could take it one day at a time. Yes. That was the best way to not get too close. She was already falling for the man. It wasn't fair to him to let things get too far without him knowing everything about her. And she wasn't ready for that. She might never be.

Her phone dinged and vibrated against the kitchen table. She jumped, spilling her coffee on her hand. Shaking her head, she stood and grabbed a towel from the counter and wiped up the mess. She picked up her phone and read the text. It was from Frank, *He didn't show for the meeting with parole officer. Will keep you posted. Stay tucked away where you are.*

Torie took a deep breath and tossed her phone back on the table. Her past wrapped around her like the blanket had, smothering and restrictive. Yes. Keeping Keith at arm's length was best.

A knock at the door brought her from her thoughts. Keith was here. She was going horseback riding. She plastered on her best smile and went to answer the door.

***

Torie answered the door with a big grin on her face but something was off. He could sense it. Bones sat next to him on the front porch wagging her tail and whining. She wanted to be near Torie. He did too.

"Come on in."

She opened the door for him and he stepped inside. Bones stayed on the front porch.

He pulled her in and hugged her. She wrapped her arms around him but wasn't relaxed. Yep. Something was definitely off.

She stepped back from his embrace. "Will I need a coat?"

He eyed her jeans, boots, and sporty long-sleeved top. "Maybe. It's getting cooler. Snow is coming in the next few days. Better safe than sorry."

"I'll be right back then."

He watched her go up the stairs and racked his brain to think of what could've happened between last night and this morning that would cause a change in her demeanor.

Her phone buzzed from the kitchen. He went and picked it up, intending to give it to her when she came downstairs. He'd noticed she tended to leave it unless it was in her pocket or purse.

As he walked back into the living room it buzzed against his hand. He looked at the screen. A text from someone name Frank popped up saying, *I wouldn't worry too much. You should be safe.*

The hair on the back of Keith's neck stood on end. She should be safe? Safe from what? Or whom? And who was Frank? A thousand thoughts ran through his head at once, distracting him from hearing Torie returning downstairs.

"Okay. I'm ready. Let's go."

Keith blinked and snapped out of it. "Here. Your phone buzzed. I got it for you..."

She took it from him, glanced at the screen, and then set it on the table by the front door. "I'll leave it here. I don't need it and wouldn't want to lose it while we're riding."

He searched her eyes. Reading the text hadn't upset her. She'd looked at it and put the phone away without a response. Was she worried about her safety? Visions of her pulling a gun on him that morning at breakfast along with her tensing over the gunshot the other day while they danced in the barn floated through his mind. He'd sensed she was spooked about something but couldn't imagine what. Now, because of this text from Frank, his mind was spinning with ideas. Torie, however, was cool as a cucumber.

"Come on, Bones. Let's go." The dog trotted along next to Torie as they headed towards his truck.

She was a tad frigid with him as well. Was this Frank a boyfriend? No. He didn't get that vibe. He did, however, get a vibe that something was definitely going on with Miss Torie Walker. He intended to find out exactly what it was.

He took one last look at the phone then closed and locked the door behind him.

* * *

Torie was grateful the drive to the barn wasn't long. Her heart was pounding so hard in her chest she feared Keith could see it through her top. And not just from the texts she'd received from Frank or the concern that Keith had read them when he'd picked up her phone, but rather from the fact that she would soon be sitting atop a horse.

Living at Gram's house in Wyoming, she'd seen plenty of horses. She even liked to sit by the fence that ran along the property not far from her Gram's mobile home and watch them as they ran through the pasture or stood in the sun, grazing. Fascinated by them, she found them to be beautiful and majestic. But adored from afar, not up close and personal.

They pulled up to the barn and got out. Bones sniffed the ground and trotted towards the barn. Keith took Torie's hand and led the way.

She'd hated pulling away from him when he hugged her. Sending mixed messages wasn't her thing and yet she'd never been so unsure of what to do. Her heart said to jump in, all in. But her head said to remember her history and not burden anyone with that. Especially not a man like Keith.

They went around the side of the barn where two horses were saddled and ready, both tied to a T-shaped post that was anchored in the ground. Torie stopped in her tracks, letting go of Keith's hand.

He turned to her. "Are you okay?"

She nodded but said, "They're really big."

He smiled. "Yes. They are. They're horses. But I promise you they are gentle as lambs. Well, Patsy is anyway."

Torie stared at him. "And which one will I be riding?"

"You'll be riding Patsy. And believe me, she's the calmest horse ever born. She's my mother's horse. We let our friends' children ride her. You'll be safe, I promise."

Torie looked at both horses. The one he called Patsy did look nice enough. The other one didn't look mean, per se, but he sure was huge. And beautiful. A dark chestnut color with a black mane and tail. "And what about that one?"

Keith walked over to the horse and rubbed its nose. "This here is Caliber. He's my horse." His face lit up as he talked. This was his element. Where he belonged.

"He's enormous."

"I'm not a small man."

Torie laughed in spite of her anxiety. "Good point."

Keith held out his hand to her. "Come on. I promise you have no reason to be afraid."

She took his hand and joined him near the horses. Patsy nudged Torie's shoulder with her nose.

"See? You can trust me."

11

TORIE LOOKED UP at Keith, her breath stolen. *Trust him*. He'd been talking about the horses, of course, but his words still hit her between the eyes. She did trust him. He'd never given her any reason not to. But with her heart? Could she let him see the broken, torn bits of it? And would he still find her loveable?

"Come on. I'll help you." He untied both horses and led them away from the barn. Torie followed, still not sure about this being a good idea. Keith came around Patsy's left side and motioned Torie to him. She obeyed. Standing next to him and the horse made her feel smaller than ever before.

"I promise, Dragonfly. You're gonna love it." He winked and gave her his best dimple-filled smile, the one that made her insides go goofy.

She nodded, words failing her.

He told her to grab the saddle horn and place her left foot in his cupped hands. She did so and in one swift movement, he hoisted her into the saddle. Hmph. Okay. It wasn't as terrifying as she originally thought. The saddle was even comfortable in its own way.

"Relax, Torie." Keith said as he patted her leg.

She took a deep breath and let her muscles loosen a bit. Patsy did the same beneath her.

"She can sense how you're feeling. Get comfy in the saddle and trust her. She'll be gentle."

Torie nodded but didn't let go of the saddle horn.

"It's okay to speak too." He teased. She caught a glimmer of his blue eyes before he ducked his head to alter the stirrups for her. His tan cowboy hat blocked his face.

Keith moved around the horse, adjusting things and tugging on straps. He handed her the reins and said, "Hold these in one hand, the other you can keep on the saddle horn. We're just walking today and Patsy will stick close to Caliber."

Torie nodded again but still couldn't find her voice.

Keith chuckled and nodded in return. "Alright then, here we go." He sauntered over to his horse, put a foot in the stirrup, then hoisted himself in the saddle, smooth as silk.

Show-off.

In jeans, a denim jacket, and cowboy hat, he was one yummy-looking show-off though. Torie decided to forgive him.

Keith clicked his tongue and Caliber started walking. Patsy fell in behind without any urging. Torie held onto the reins in one hand, the saddle horn in the other, and tried to acclimate herself to the motion. They crossed the property and headed for a path that led into the trees. So far, so good.

"You doing okay back there?" Keith said over his shoulder.

She nodded.

"I can't hear you nod, Dragonfly."

Right. Oops. "I'm fine." Oh good. Her voice did still work.

Keith's laughter floated back to her, filling the air with a sense of calm. Torie found the tension inside her uncurling with every step Patsy took. She let her body flow naturally with the sway of Patsy's steps, their movements syncing together. As they moved through the trees, Torie soaked in the sights and sounds around her. The clomp of the horse's hooves on the dirt path, the breeze rustling through the tops of the trees, and the branches sweeping along Keith's jacket sleeve, then hers, as they passed. Bones serpentined back and forth, trotting through the trees and stopping to sniff here and there. Doggy heaven.

The trees opened up into a clearing, allowing Patsy to move up alongside Caliber.

Torie sighed.

"That sounded good," Keith said, smiling at her from

under his hat.

"What sounded good?"

"That sigh."

Had she sighed?

He looked forward again, the two horses moseying along now side by side.

"It's so beautiful here. I can see why you love it."

Keith nodded but didn't say anything.

"And I understand why you love riding too." She leaned forward in the saddle and patted Patsy's neck. "They're such gorgeous animals. Big—which is why I was nervous. But you're right. She's a sweetheart."

"Told ya."

"Yeah, yeah, I hear ya. Just trust you, I know."

"Do you trust me?" Keith's face was serious now. All signs of teasing gone.

"Yes. I do." She answered without hesitation.

"So, it's your control issue that's the problem." His teasing tone was back.

"I believe that's a pot-meet-kettle situation if I ever heard one, Captain."

He laughed. "Fair enough. You do have to give up some control to ride. Trust the horse, work with him instead of against him."

"Is that why you love training them?"

"Partly. I think it's also because many horses haven't had trainers or riders who develop a relationship with them."

"Okay. You're gonna have to explain that one."

Keith had one hand resting on his thigh, the other holding Caliber's reins loose over the saddle horn. The man looked like he was born in a saddle. "Too many riders treat horses like big, dumb animals. Try to force them to do what the rider wants. But if you get to know a horse, get a sense for his spirit, you can work with him. Learn to read each other."

Torie had a feeling Keith wasn't just talking about horses. In the same way Aimee misunderstood him at first, Torie guessed most people saw Keith as big and dangerous without taking the time to really know him.

The walked along a bit further in quiet. Caliber took the lead once more as they wove through another patch of trees. Torie looked to her right and saw a cabin about fifty yards away in a small clearing.

"What is that?"

Keith looked. "That's my place."

Oh.

Torie was aware he lived on the property but hadn't wondered until now exactly what his house would look like. It was bigger than Dane and Aimee's, with a front and back porch that didn't wrap around. It sat up a little on a small hill, a log fence surrounding it. An enormous stone chimney took up over half of one side, a wagon wheel leaning against it. Made entirely of huge logs, it epitomized the word cabin and everything about it was Keith. Impressive, yet warm once you got a bit closer.

"Wow."

"Thanks."

Apparently, he wasn't ready to stop and show her around, because they kept moving through the trees and away from his cabin. Fair enough. He was a private man. Torie could respect that. And it was a reminder she needed to keep some distance between them anyway. Her heart sank at the thought.

Patsy moved up next to Caliber again once they reached another clearing.

"I built it myself."

Keith's deep voice cut through the quiet.

It took Torie a second to realize he was talking about his cabin.

"Seriously? That's impressive."

He shrugged. "I like to build things."

"Ah, the old Lincoln Log obsession."

He grunted. "Obsession is a bit much."

She wagged a finger at him. "You're just irked your mom let that cat out of the bag." She winked at him. "Don't worry though. Your secret is safe with me."

He laughed, his whole body moving in the saddle. "It's not really a secret that I like to build."

"You don't like to talk about it though. But you should. You do incredible work. Take some pride in that, Captain."

"I don't like the attention. Don't need it."

"Really? You?" Her voice dripped with sarcasm.

He shook his head.

"I would love to see it sometime. Your cabin." Good Lord. That sounded like a line. She tried to recover. "I mean...it's really a beautiful house. I bet the inside is as nice as the outside." Okay, the earth could open up and swallow her whole now. Anytime...

Keith chuckled, aware of her discomfort. "I'm good with that. I would've stopped today but...well, it's not too tidy at the moment." Now it was his turn to blush with embarrassment.

"Ah, the bachelor pad problem. I hear ya."

His smile fell just a tad. Barely noticeable, but Torie caught it.

"You seem to be doing fine in the saddle."

Change of subject. Fair enough.

"Yeah. I think I'm catching on pretty well. You may make a full-on cowgirl of me yet."

***

Torie's grin mixed with her golden hair flowing in the breeze was not lost on Keith.

He meant it too. She took to the saddle without issue. Well, as soon as she relaxed enough to stop gripping the saddle horn like a vice and moved along with Patsy. He noticed when she released control of a situation, her eyes lit up and the weight she carried on her shoulders fell away.

He'd wanted to take her riding, to give her an adventure, something she'd never done before. But also to experience the freedom riding brought. It was one of the main reasons he loved being on horseback so much. It was one of the few places he was truly free.

As peaceful as their ride was, Keith couldn't shake his concern over the text he saw on her phone. Torie didn't seem too concerned, certainly not since she literally decided to sit back and enjoy the ride. But he was. There was a whole lot about Torie Walker he wanted to know—needed to know. And he was going to find out.

"So, you wanna tell me about what happened last night?"

His mind deep in thought over Torie's safety, her question caught him off guard. "What?"

She rode beside him, a cautious look in her eye. "I'm not slow. There was more going on between you and Clint than him just being a jerk. A married jerk, apparently, which makes him even creepier."

Keith's stomach turned. He grunted.

"That's not much of an answer, Captain."

She'd turned the tables on him. He wanted to know more about her, so it was only fair she wanted the same from him. But God help him, he wasn't sure he was ready to open that Pandora's box just yet. Not with Torie. He liked her too much. Which scared the hell out of him. He couldn't take his heart tearing up any more than it already had. Torie rejecting him could quite possibly do him in.

"We went to high school together." He offered that nugget of info. Maybe she'd chew on that and be satisfied.

"Okay. And?"

Maybe not.

"We played football together."

She looked over at him and rolled her eyes. "Seriously? You think you can give me 'we went to high school together and played football' and I'm gonna believe that's all that's between you? I saw you, Keith. Your eyes and body language spoke volumes."

They'd known each other such a short time and already she could read him like a book. Sure, it hadn't been hard to see he was upset with Clint for grabbing her like he did, but Torie recognized something more. Something deeper. And damn it if she wasn't right. She just had no clue *how* right she was.

He took a deep breath. "Let's just say he caused some trouble for me in the past."

"Nope. Still not enough to make me happy."

Oh man, every fiber in his being wanted nothing more than to make her happy, but not by spilling his life story. He wasn't ready for that yet. And he didn't think she was either.

"How about I tell you more about Clint if you tell me who Frank is." It was out of his mouth before he could filter it from his brain, but he didn't regret it. She wanted to know about his past? He wanted to know about her present.

Her jaw dropped and she gave him the evil eye. "You *did*

look at my phone!"

He shrugged. He felt bad about it, but not that bad. If Torie was in danger, he sure as hell wanted to know about it.

"I knew it." She shook her head. "You're nosy. You're a nosy Hulk."

He couldn't help it, he burst out laughing. "You're stalling, Walker. And call me that nickname again and you're gonna have bigger problems than Frank to deal with."

Her face and shoulders fell, her indignant demeanor switching off like a light.

"Hey, I'm sorry." He reached out and rubbed her arm. His heart pleaded with God—please don't let Frank be a boyfriend, *please don't let Frank be a boyfriend...*

She attempted a smile. "No. It's okay." With a sigh, she looked up at the trees, her body swaying along with Patsy's footsteps.

"Frank is a friend from the police force. Sort of a father figure to me, really."

Good. Not a boyfriend. Father figure he could handle.

He waited. Gave her time to continue. They were almost back to the barn. She was talking, letting him in a little. But he needed more. "And who is Frank telling you not to worry about?"

She looked down at her hands. She'd let go of the saddle horn, the reins resting between her fingers. They were unnecessary at this point, really. Patsy didn't need much guidance. Her fingers fidgeted with one another. She was debating how much to tell him. She trusted him, but not with everything. Not yet. But could he blame her? He'd only given her the tip of his life's iceberg.

The barn came into view and the horses walked a tad faster. The knowledge of fresh hay and water always spurred them towards home. Patsy's quicker pace made Torie sit up and grab the saddle horn again.

"We're back."

Keith nodded, disappointed their conversation was over. She was close to telling him who or what she was hiding from. But pushing her wasn't what he wanted.

The horses walked up to the side of the barn and stopped.

"They really do seem to know the way, don't they?" Torie said as Keith climbed off Caliber and helped her down from Patsy's saddle.

"Yes ma'am, they do." Keith held onto Torie as she slid down Patsy's side and to the ground. Her knees wobbled a bit beneath her. He held her waist tight, pulling her a tad closer than necessary to hold her upright. She looked up at him, her hazel eyes soft, her hands up against his chest. Her mouth was so close, her breath a mix of mint and something sweet. He couldn't help it, he had to have a taste. Lowering his lips to hers, he kissed her soft and slow. Her hands moved up around his neck. Her fingers danced across his skin, making his blood heat and his body want more.

Patsy stomped a foot, pulling them back to earth. It was

a good thing too. Keith had promised Torie self-control. A kiss like that would test any man's ability to hold back.

Torie's hand floated down to his biceps as she leaned her forehead into his chest. She took a deep breath and let it out.

"I know what you mean, Dragonfly."

She looked up at him, those gorgeous eyes now fighting back tears. "My dad. My dad is the one Frank is warning me about."

12

KEITH TRIED NOT to alter his grip on Torie but he couldn't help it. Whether to keep them both upright or because his first instinct was to get her as close to him as possible, he wasn't sure, but he wrapped his arms around her, one hand holding her head against his chest.

Good Lord, what had this woman been through? His mind raced in a thousand directions as he held her tight. Her body moved with the tears that now flowed, sobs muffled against his shirt. His heart ached for her as she let out what must've been years of pent-up emotion. Such a strong woman. Tough on the outside, warm and gentle on the inside. His Dragonfly, was right.

He had no clue how long they stood there but he didn't

care. He'd hold her forever, let her cry until she collapsed if that's what would make her world better. Thoughts of wringing her father's neck with his bare hands flashed through his mind but he pushed those away. Torie needed him. And he needed her. He'd walk to the ends of the earth for this woman. He loved her. Sure, he could tell himself otherwise, but he'd be lying.

He'd figure out how to handle that revelation later. For now, the precious woman in his arms was his main focus. Her breathing settled and although his shirt was soaked, she wasn't crying as much anymore.

She pulled back a bit and wiped her face. "Oh...I'm sorry about your shirt." She swiped at the wet spots as if that would dry them up.

He bent down to look her square in the eye. Those lonely, hazel depths, red rimmed and full of tears grabbed hold of him and melted his heart. "Don't worry about my shirt. It'll dry just fine."

She nodded and looked down, her hands still flat against his chest. He took them in his and kissed each one. He pulled her to him once more, her arms wrapped around his waist inside his coat. His bulk engulfed her as he held her once more. The lemon scent of her hair filled his senses.

She took a deep breath and sighed, her body now almost limp against his. How long had she gone without having someone to lean on? Had she *ever* had anyone to lean on?

So many questions swirled in his head without answers.

But there would be time for those later. Right now, his only task was taking care of Torie. She sniffed and took a step back, wiping her face with both hands.

"Sheesh. I'm so sorry. I *never* lose it like that. Honestly."

He could see her struggling to put up the wall she was so used to keeping in place. The one that said she could handle anything on her own. No help needed. That was the last thing he wanted.

"Don't apologize. Maybe you should lose it more often."

She gave him a weak smile and wiped her nose with the back of her hand. "Ugh. Man. I am seriously a mess."

"There's a small washroom in the back of the barn, right near the workout area. You can use that to clean up if you want. I'll just get the horses put away. Take your time."

She nodded. "Thanks."

She brushed past him and into the barn. Keith took off his hat and ran a hand through his hair. He put his hat back on and started taking Patsy's saddle off, yanking on the straps with more force than necessary. Adrenaline pumped through his veins at the thought of anyone touching a hair on Torie's head.

She'd said her dad was abusive and that she went to live with her gram after her mother died, but she never mentioned what happened to her father. Why hadn't Keith caught on to that? And why would she be in danger from him?

Torie came out of the washroom and sat on a hay bale as Keith finished putting the horses away. She'd offered to help but he said no. He could tell she was exhausted. He hadn't realized just how worked up she was about horseback riding until this morning and then the meltdown over her dad only added insult to injury. Guilt tore at him over not seeing her angst about riding. It had all worked out the way he figured it would, but he had no idea just how much was lurking under the surface for her.

Well, he was aware now.

Bones sat next to her on the hay bale, doggy bliss written all over her face as Torie rubbed the dog's head and back. She'd reach over and lick Torie's cheek every few minutes. Cheeks salty from tears, no doubt. God bless that dog. She'd been his comfort too many times to count. He was grateful now she stuck close to Torie.

With the horses washed down and back in their stalls, Keith tucked Torie into his truck and drove her back to Dane and Aimee's cabin. Bones rode in the truck bed. Keith figured Torie would want to go inside, lock the door, and not come out for days, so he was pleasantly surprised when she said, "Do you wanna come in for a bit? I could make us some lunch."

It wasn't an invitation to hear her entire story, but it was an invitation he most definitely wasn't going to turn down.

"I'd love that. Why don't you go on in and get showered and changed. I'll go to my place and do the same. Meet you back here in about half an hour?"

She looked down at her jeans and smiled. "Good call.

Horse smell is…unique."

"It certainly is." He took her hand in his and kissed it. "See you in a few."

She nodded and climbed out of the truck. He waited and watched until she was inside before he drove away.

* * *

Torie wiped the condensation from the bathroom mirror. Her eyes were still a bit red from crying, but the puffiness for the most part was gone. Thank God. And the horse smell was replaced with a soapy scent mixed with her lemon-scented shampoo.

She threw on some old, comfy jeans with tears in the knees and her favorite sweatshirt. It was gray with SDPD written across the front in blue. It was huge and soft and enveloped her like a treasured childhood blanket. Pulling her wet hair into a clip, she looked at her reflection and groaned.

Normally if a guy were coming over to hang out with her, she'd have her best outfit on and her hair perfect. But this wasn't just any guy. This was Keith. A man who didn't give one hoot what she was wearing or how much makeup she had on. And quite frankly, she'd never had a guy in her life okay with just hanging out. It was refreshing, really. She could be herself with Keith. Truly herself. Enough of herself to have a total breakdown in his arms.

She shook her head and moved to the kitchen to make

their lunch. Rummaging through the fridge, she pulled out deli meat, cheese, tomato, and pickle. Had she really totally lost it on him? Crying like a baby into his shirt? Ugh! She cringed as she laid out sandwich fixings on the counter. She was tougher than that. She'd pushed through so much in her life, proved herself over and over again. Why did she let her guard down with Keith?

Her heart knew but her head wanted to fight it. Her head argued it wasn't fair to get involved with someone like Keith. He could never forgive her or get past who she really was. But her heart said she wouldn't know unless she tried. Keith was more real with her than anyone had ever been. He'd shown her in a mere few days how it felt to be cared for. Cared about. Dare she say cherished? It was all so new to her. No one had ever taken an interest in her. Not beyond how she looked on their arm anyway. But Keith was different. Different in so many ways.

She slathered mayonnaise and mustard onto six pieces of wheat bread. She wasn't sure exactly how Keith liked his sandwiches but from what she'd seen of him so far at meals, he wasn't a picky eater. And she figured it was safe to start with two sandwiches for him instead of one.

She smiled as she pieced together each sandwich, cut them in half, and placed them on plates. He was a big boy, that was certain. Her heartbeat sped up at the memory of his kiss. One minute he was helping her down from Patsy's saddle, the next he was kissing her senseless. Her legs had been wobbly from the horseback ride, after that she could hardly stand. But his arms held her tight. Safe. Supported. Keith was a man she could lean on.

Looking out the kitchen window, she whispered a short prayer. She was tired. Tired of being afraid. Tired of keeping everything to herself. Tired of living her life alone. She would tell Keith her story. She'd tell him the truth about her. And let the chips fall where they may. It was a risk, yes, but one she was ready to take.

She added pretzels to their plates and placed them on the kitchen table with napkins and two glasses of ice water. Perfect. She turned her head towards the door at Keith's knock. It was now or never. With a deep breath, she headed to the living room and opened the door.

* * *

Keith knocked on the door and waited. He had no clue what state Torie would be in since she'd let herself cry it out on his shoulder. Well, chest. His shirt held buckets worth of her tears, it would surely take a week to dry. But Torie's heart? That was another matter entirely. Would that ever mend? And would she be willing to let him help her try?

He heard her footfalls against the wood floor behind the door. She opened it and leaned against it, one bare foot stacked up on the other. Her toenails were painted a bright blue. Man, even her feet were gorgeous. He took in the sight of her for a moment. She wore an old SDPD sweatshirt and torn jeans. Her wet hair was twisted up in one of those clip things that looked more like an element of torture than a hair accessory. No makeup, no fuss. Just her. She'd never looked more beautiful.

"Hey." Her voice was almost a whisper.

"Hey yourself. You doin' okay?"

"Yeah. Come on in." She motioned him inside and closed the door behind him after he entered.

"I whipped up some sandwiches from some stuff I bought at the store the other day. Is that all right? I wasn't sure exactly what you like so I guessed."

She looked nervous. Vulnerable. It was a new side to her. One he liked. It meant she trusted him.

"I'm a man. I'll take a good sandwich any way I can get it." He winked at her. She smiled. Mission accomplished.

He followed her into the kitchen. The table was set with two place settings, each one holding a plate filled with pretzels and a sandwich. Well, his held two sandwiches. He grinned. Yet another reason to fall for this woman. They both took a seat and Keith said a short blessing over the meal.

They ate in quiet for a few minutes, Keith not wanting to push her to talk if she didn't want to. He loved her company. Loved that she didn't feel the need to fill silences, was just content to be together. He was quickly seeing all the things he loved about Torie and it scared him less and less. She was a tough woman. Maybe she *could* handle living in his world. But he was putting the cart way before the horse. There was still obviously a lot he didn't know about her yet, and he'd been rather private about his life as well. They'd have to move through that if they wanted any kind of future together.

One step at a time.

Torie took a swig of water and a then a deep breath. "I really am sorry I lost it on you after our ride. It was such a beautiful morning, and I had to go and ruin it with my meltdown."

Keith shook his head. "You didn't ruin anything. And you're right. It was a beautiful morning."

She nodded in agreement. "I guess you're probably wanting to know more about my dad now."

"I want to listen to whatever you want to tell me." And he meant it too. He would never push her. Ever. He knew better than anyone what it was like to have gut wrenching memories tear at you, scenes from war that no one should have to carry. He retreated like a bear to its cave when people tried to push him about what he'd seen and done as a soldier. The last thing he ever wanted was to make Torie feel that way.

She took another deep breath and placed her wadded-up napkin on her plate. She'd picked at her sandwich, only finishing half of it along with about two pretzels.

"I told you my dad was abusive. And he was." Tears sat on the edge of her lashes, threatening to fall. They didn't. Just stayed there, a shiny veil in front of the hurt that lurked behind.

"My parents were from a small town in Colorado. They met in high school. Mom was a beauty pageant queen, of all things. Turned heads wherever we went."

Keith sat with his arms resting on the table on either side of his plate. He'd devoured both sandwiches and now listened with rapt attention to every word Torie spoke. Seeing the beauty that sat across from him, it made perfect sense her mother had been a stunner. That DNA was definitely passed on.

"Dad was your stereotypical small-town boy. Outgoing and popular. Captain of the football team, Mom was head cheerleader, etc., etc. Anyway, they married after high school and had my brother then me."

Keith kept his face like stone, unmoving and not responding to the news that she had a brother. His mind, however, spun like a pinwheel. She had said she had "no siblings to speak of." Must've meant the brother wasn't worth mentioning.

Torie looked away from him and out the kitchen window. "He began hitting my mom not long after they were married. From their arguments, I gathered it was his way of controlling her. Or trying to, anyway. She had men look at her all the time. My dad couldn't stand it. Said she asked for it, flaunted herself to the men in town. She didn't, of course, but he knew she wouldn't leave the house after a beating. Didn't want the world to see proof of her own private hell. He started abusing me when I was about twelve."

A tear drifted down Torie's cheek and landed in her lap.

"You really don't need to continue, Torie. I get the idea."

She looked straight at him, the pain in her eyes tearing a hole in his gut.

"No. I need you to know the whole story."

He nodded. She continued.

"My brother became a drug addict and left when I was fourteen. Just before it all happened."

"What happened?"

"My dad killed my mom and he blames me for it."

13

KEITH'S MIND WAS racing before Torie started talking. Now it was in a tailspin that made him almost dizzy. Had he heard her correctly?

Reading his thoughts, Torie said, "You heard me right. Let's go into the living room where it's more comfortable."

Keith nodded and followed her into the other room but still couldn't find his voice. Or a single damn thing to say. She could've knocked him over with a feather after that revelation.

They settled in on the couch together, Torie turned sideways to face him, one of her mile-long legs tucked underneath her. Her hands sat folded in her lap, one hand toying with her fingernails on the other. He recognized her

MO when she was nervous.

He took her right hand in his and held it tight. "You can tell me as much or as little as you want, Torie."

She propped her elbow on the back of the couch and leaned her head on her hand. "No. I want to tell you. I've never told anyone. I think it's time."

He kissed her hand then enveloped it in both of his. He needed to be close to her, feel as if he was protecting her somehow.

"After my brother left, my mom was a mess. Her world was spinning out of control. My dad was a loaded gun, we never knew when he'd go off. She'd tried to get my brother off drugs, but it was no use. It was his escape from our world. He tried to protect my mom and took some good beatings for it, but in the end, he just couldn't stay."

"Did your mom and brother know what your dad was doing to you?" Saying the words out loud made Keith's blood boil. He decided right then and there if he ever came across Torie's father, the man wouldn't leave the room alive.

"Not at first. I was ashamed and thought she'd be mad at me."

Keith squeezed her hand then wiped a tear that slid down her face.

"She eventually figured it out. Thankfully, she wasn't mad at me. It ended up being the last straw and what motivated her to leave him."

"She was planning on leaving him?"

Torie nodded. "She mapped out a plan of how to sneak away. He was crazy diligent in how he kept track of her, but she thought she'd found away around it. We were going to go live with Gram."

"What happened?"

"My dad found out. He came after me, saying it was all my fault she wanted to go. Mom stepped in, tried to protect me. When she did, he threw her across the room. She landed on a glass table. Died instantly."

Keith pulled Torie into his lap and held her. She tucked her face into his neck and sobbed. She could soak every damn shirt he owned if it helped her heal. Even in the craziest corners of his imagination, he never could've come up with the story she just told him. Never.

Torie pulled back and looked at him. "I have to tell you the rest."

A strand of her hair had come loose from her clip. He gently tucked it behind her ear.

"No, Dragonfly. You don't."

"I do. Believe it or not, this is helping. To unload all this feels...right. I'm just sorry to unload it all on you."

He grazed her forehead with his lips. "I'm not. I'm honored you chose me to share this with. You've carried it alone for way too long."

She nodded and crawled out of his lap but sat next to him with her legs draped over his, his hands resting on her knees.

She continued her story right where she'd left off. "I ran. Hauled it to the neighbor's house. I couldn't speak, but the whole town knew what my dad was like. The woman took one look at my face and called the police. Dad was carried off to jail and I was sent to live with Gram."

She took a deep breath, let it out again. "Flash forward to years later. I changed my last name, took my mother's maiden name, became a cop, and have kept track of my dad ever since. Frank helps me keep an eye on him. I guess he knows the whole story, but that's it. My brother contacts me from time to time. He has my cell number. Knows I'll help him if I can, but since I won't give him money, we don't talk often."

Keith rubbed his hands along her legs, a gesture of comfort to her but more of a need for him to touch her, know for his own peace of mind she was okay. Physically, anyway. Sitting there listening to her story made emotions run through him he didn't know he had. He couldn't imagine her carrying this alone all these years.

"So why is Frank worried for you now?"

"All this time Dad's been in prison. He couldn't get to me. However, due to a technicality, he just made parole and didn't show for the meeting with his parole officer. No one knows where he is."

The hair on the back of Keith's neck stood on end. "And what makes Frank, or you, think you might be in danger?"

"Like I said, he blames me for my mom's death. Says it's

because of me he lost her. It should've been me who died that day. He wants me dead.

* * *

Torie watched as Keith absorbed all she was throwing at him. Even a guy as tough as Keith would have a hard time digesting her story. Sheesh. It was *her* story and she still had trouble believing it herself. At times, that portion of her life felt like a dream. At other times, the more vivid memories were a nightmare.

Keith's jaw twitched. His hands were on her legs, holding on as if he couldn't let her go. Oh, how she wished that were true. After all she'd just laid on him, she wouldn't be surprised if he hightailed it and ran without a single glance back.

Steeling herself for his reply, she tucked her heart in tight and waited for the blow. Instead, he lifted her chin, a tender gesture for such a force of a man. "Look at me, Dragonfly."

She did. And got lost in a sea of blue full of concern and…love? Her heart didn't dare think it, let alone believe it. Someone like Keith could never love someone like her.

"I'm so sorry. Sorry you've carried all this pain alone for so long. Sorry for what that bastard of a father did to you." He shook his head and took a deep breath. "But I will do everything in my power to keep you safe. From this moment on, anyone who even *thinks* about trying to hurt you is going to have to go through me."

He cupped her face and drew her to him. He placed the softest of kisses on her lips, then moved to her cheeks and then her eyes, ending with a tender brush of his lips on her forehead.

Oh yes. Cherished is how this man made her feel.

Her face still in his hands, he placed his forehead to hers and closed his eyes. Between a slow deep breath and the slight tremor she felt moving through him, she sensed him fighting for control. She understood it all too well. Many times she lay in bed at night, unable to sleep, thinking only of what it would be like to rid the world of her dad. But never had she experienced someone wanting to do so in her defense.

Keith wasn't the kind of man who'd go looking for trouble. However, he'd defend to the death anyone he cared about. She'd seen that first hand when Aimee had been in trouble. And he cared for Torie enough to do the same.

With each word Torie had spoken to Keith, the burden of all the years of holding it all in, carrying it all herself, fell from her shoulders. He hadn't turned away from her, but rather said he would gladly step in front of her, protect her. Be there for her. Whether he actually loved her or not, she had no clue. But this... What this man offered her now, was enough. More than enough.

She pulled back and held both his hands in hers. "Thank you. Thank you for listening and for not..." She turned towards the fireplace, unable to look him in the eye.

He gently brought her face back square with his. "For not what?"

She blinked, willing away more tears. "Not walking away from me."

His brow furrowed and he pulled her into his lap again. Oh, how that was quickly becoming a favorite spot of hers. He wrapped his arms around her and held her close. She tucked into his chest, accepting his warmth.

"Now, why would I go and do a stupid thing like that?"

Unable to help it, she laughed. This man truly had no idea how amazing he was. How unique.

One of his arms wrapped around her waist. He lifted the other and unclipped her hair. He placed the clip beside them on the couch and stroked her hair. His lips settled against the top of her head and stayed there.

"I love the smell of your hair." His voice was muffled as he nuzzled close to her ear, sending shivers all over her body. "Like fresh lemons in the summer."

She smiled and placed a soft kiss on his neck. A low growl rumbled in his chest.

"You're gonna drive me crazy, woman."

She looked up into his eyes and laughed. "Sorry. Well, not really."

He laughed as well, but then his demeanor became serious again. "I want to make sure you hear me, Torie. I don't ever say anything I don't mean."

There was not a doubt in her mind that was the truth.

Keith thought before he spoke. Always. This man was self-control personified. It was unlike anything she'd ever seen before, really.

"I won't ever turn away from you. And I will do everything in my power to protect you."

"Even though I'm…" She buried her head in his chest once more.

He rubbed her back. "Even though you're what? Beautiful inside and out? Willing to let me be quiet and broody without giving me grief?"

She wanted to smile but couldn't. "No. Because I'm not…perfect. My dad, he took from me…" The tears started again and man, if that didn't piss her off. She was done with tears. Done shedding them over her dad.

Keith held her tight and stroked her hair again. "I understand all your dad took from you, Dragonfly. And believe me when I say I'd like to explain to the man myself all the wrong there is in his choices. But God makes you whole again. I promise you that. And as far as perfect? Who is? We're all a mess. Just trying to do our best while praying God can use the broken pieces in some way."

"How could God ever forgive all I've done? I haven't exactly made the best choices with my life."

"Oh, sweet woman. He can. I'm living proof of that."

She looked up at him. "What do you mean?"

He looked straight towards the fireplace and didn't answer. Not right away. She leaned against his chest again, content to just be. Be held. Held by this man who cared so much for her.

When he did answer her, his chest rumbled beneath her cheek, his voice sad. "I think we've had enough stories for one day. Maybe someday soon, I'll tell you mine." He kissed the top of her head. "For now, I wanna focus on you."

No one had ever taken so much interest in her. The real her. She liked the sound of that. She took a deep breath and relaxed completely in Keith's arms. Yes. This was most definitely her favorite place to be.

* * *

Keith could tell the moment Torie drifted off the sleep. Her breathing became even and her body melted against his, all tension gone. However, he was wound up tighter than a drum. Between his attraction to the beautiful woman now asleep in his arms and the rage he battled to control over hearing what her dad did to her, he was a mess.

He played her story over and over again in his mind. Un-friggin' believable. Keith was a soldier. Marine Corps Force Recon. And yet what Torie had just laid on him could rank up there with some of the worst crap he'd ever seen or heard of in his time of service.

Where was her brother? She said he took off, but was she afraid he would come after her in some way too? Maybe not. He couldn't take the heat of their home life so he bailed.

Unlikely he'd have any desire to hurt Torie. But if he knew where Torie was, would he help her dad find her?

Questions swirled in his head, making him want to get up immediately and build a wall around the property eight miles high and three miles thick. Now he understood Torie's need to construct walls around herself, emotionally and otherwise. She couldn't trust a damn soul.

He looked down at her, sleeping like a child in his arms. No, not a child. A full grown, gorgeous woman who trusted him enough to share her entire story, even though she feared he'd walk away from her after having heard it.

He laid his head against the back of the sofa and settled deeper into the cushions. He'd stay here all day and all night if it meant she got decent sleep and felt safe. Who cared if his arms lost feeling? As long as they were wrapped around her, he was content.

When he mentioned he was living proof that God can make someone whole, she'd asked what he meant. And man, did everything in him want to spill his guts. Share his demons too. But the day was already heavy ladened enough with crap from her past, he didn't need to add his to the mix as well.

Part of that was true and yet part of him had to admit he was also afraid. She'd laid it all on the line with him, risking his rejection. Was he brave enough to do the same? Trust her with his heart as she'd trusted him?

He placed a whisper of a kiss on her forehead and prayed. Prayed he had the courage to tell her all of his past mistakes. And prayed she could see beyond them to maybe give them a chance together.

He had Torie in his arms. And although he tried to fight it, she'd made her way into his heart as well. He just hoped she'd let him into hers as well

14

TORIE HOPPED OUT Torie of the shower and finished getting dressed. She was meeting Rae for lunch and some shopping and was already running late. She and Keith had worked out that morning. After yesterday they both had some angst to work through. And with telling Keith everything, it was as if a hundred-pound pack was lifted off her back. It didn't change the fact that her dad was still out there somewhere, but she didn't have to face anything alone anymore.

She'd fallen asleep in Keith's arms and woke up in them as well. The poor man. Sat there and held her for hours. He'd dozed off as well, his snoring what woke her. She had to stifle a laugh when he'd stood and walked funny because both his legs tingled from having fallen asleep. He didn't complain though.

They'd talked a bit more. Nothing special. Just about horses and what she liked about her job. He'd cooked up some pasta for them for dinner then made sure she was tucked into the cabin, safe and sound, before he left for the evening. Exhausted from her day, amazing nap or not, she had hunkered down by a cozy fire Keith built for her in her room before he left, and read Aimee's Bible some more until she fell asleep.

Keith was busy all day helping his mom get ready for the big, annual Scott Christmas party that was happening the next night, so Torie wouldn't see him. She could tell he didn't like that idea, his protective instincts detectable from space at this point, but he trusted she could take care of herself and was glad to hear she'd be with Rae most of the day. Keith had asked if he could let Tony in on some of his concerns, and she was fine with that. He wouldn't betray her trust, merely let Tony know what was necessary.

A pang of guilt hit her. Part of the reason she'd never told anyone about her dad was she didn't want anyone else affected by his madness. She'd avoided getting too close to people for a lot of reasons. Protecting them was one.

Her phone dinged on the bathroom counter while she finished applying a bit of makeup. A text from Keith that said *You okay?*

She smiled. Did the man have a sixth sense about her?

She wouldn't be surprised. They were connected in a way she couldn't explain. Her thoughts always on him. His apparently on her as well.

Yes. Just want to be sure I don't cause Tony and Rae any trouble.

Her instincts for so long had been to keep people out. Not tell them what she was thinking. With Keith, there was no hesitation. She wanted him to know everything. Even her worry over how her situation might affect his friends.

Don't worry about them. I've given Tony need-to-know intel. You and Rae are safe.

Torie wasn't exactly sure what he meant by that, but trusted him, and for the first time in her life accepted the help being offered. Keith and Tony were Special Forces Marines. They were well aware of how to protect the ones they love.

Love. Keith hadn't said the words to her, but his actions spoke volumes. He definitely cared for her, of that she had no doubt. Her phone dinged again.

Have fun today. Enjoy a nice lunch and shopping. Tahoe City is beautiful at Christmas. Wish I could join you. I've gotta help Mom with about 8,000 twinkle lights. Pray for me...

She tapped out her answer and hit send.

There's no way I believe that you'd rather go shopping.

His answer made her laugh out loud.

My mom. 8,000 twinkle lights. Southern woman throwing a huge party. I rest my case... I would gladly shop AND hold your purse.

The time on her phone glared at her. Ah! She was way beyond late now. She tapped out a quick last text to him.

I'm running super late. Gotta go. I'd love to have you with me too. And for the record, I will NEVER make you hold my purse. Ever.

Torie brushed her hair and dabbed on some lip gloss. All good. One last text came in from Keith.

God bless you for that, sweet woman. I'll check in with you later. Have a good time.

Torie grinned and tucked her phone in the back pocket of her jeans. She shook her head. Her dad was out there somewhere looking for her, she knew, and yet at the moment, she was happier than she'd ever been. Go figure.

Keith had her back. As much as she experienced that through the camaraderie of those she worked with on the police force, this was personal. No one had ever watched out for her. Not since Gram. And not like this.

She'd spoken to Frank earlier that morning on the phone. There was still no news but he liked hearing she was somewhere hidden, a place her dad probably wouldn't link to her. She knew better than anyone her dad could find her, but she'd done everything within her power to not make it easy for him.

Confident she was good for now, she double-checked her gun in her purse, grabbed her keys, and headed out the door. She mainly did girl days with Aimee but it had been a while. And Rae was fun. Today would be a good day.

* * *

Keith swore under his breath. He was on his parents' back porch, hunched over a ball of twinkle lights that were twisted in a knot. How in the name of all that was holy did his mother manage to get them this tangled? The woman was meticulous and crazy organized and yet every year she dumped the lights into one big box, stating "I'll deal with those next year." Funny thing was, she was never the one to "deal with them." It was always Keith. Or his dad, who had mysteriously disappeared into the house right around the time the box of lights appeared.

Coward.

His texting conversation with Torie earlier floated through his mind. He was absolutely positive that shopping with her *and* holding her purse would be a thousand times better than this. Hell, he'd carry *her* around if it meant getting him out of this chore. Hmph. That idea sounded appealing.

"What are you grinning about over there, Son?" His mother's voice snapped him back to his own personal twinkle light twisted nightmare. Had he been grinning? Oh yes. The thought of carrying Torie around, having her in his arms any way he could get her, had made him grin like an idiot. And he didn't care.

That was new.

Come to think it, he was experiencing a lot of new things since Torie rolled into his life. For one thing, she was on his mind all the time. Seriously. All the time. He couldn't look toward the barn now without thinking about their workouts.

How she pushed herself. Pushed him. How he laughed for the first time ever while doing push-ups because she kept teasing him that Captain America had to work on keeping up his image.

"Push-ups make you awesome. Captain America is awesome. Keep working at it. You'll get there," she'd said. All while doing about a hundred reps herself right next to him. The woman was relentless. And man, if he didn't love that about her.

That's right. He'd said it. Love. That was another thing new since Torie worked her way into his heart. He was in love with someone again. No. Not again. He'd never loved like this before. Not even Mandy. His heart sank a bit to admit that. But he'd prayed about it so much, God knew every facet of that situation. How Keith had done everything in his power to make things work.

No. His feelings for Torie were different. Much different. He just hoped that once she heard all about his past, she wouldn't change how she felt about him. He decided last night as he'd drifted off to sleep that he'd talk to her soon, but after Christmas. He wanted to enjoy the time with her, make sure her holiday was special. Not bog it down with his past.

He also wanted to focus on her sorry excuse for a father. He sure as hell wanted that idiot behind bars again, and out of Torie's life, as soon as possible. He'd made a call that morning to a friend of his in the military to see if he could put out feelers on her dad, help find him in any way. Keith would use everything possible within his power to get this situation over and done with.

He didn't notice his mother sitting on the chair beside him until she spoke. "Now your brain is traveling faster than a freight train. You wanna talk about it?" She patted the chair beside her.

He rose, walked to the chair, and sat down, accepting her invitation. Even though getting grilled by his mom wasn't his idea of a fun afternoon, it was hands down better than dealing with those stupid lights for a bit.

Keith's mother smiled at him. Her silver hair hung to her shoulders in waves. She usually wore it up in a band or clip of some kind, but today it was down. She didn't wear much makeup. Ellie Scott was the stereotypical southern woman in many ways but in others, far from it. No big hair for her. Soft and natural described his mother. Always perfectly put together, yes, but you got what you saw. Much like Torie in many ways. Steel Magnolias they were.

"Things seem to be going well between you and Torie."

And there it was.

Keith smiled in spite of himself. "Yeah. Things are going well."

"You like her."

It wasn't a question.

"I like her."

His mom nodded. "That's good. I like her too."

"Oh yeah?" Keith lifted a brow and looked at his mom.

"Don't give me that look. I realize we haven't known her long, but I've had a feeling about her ever since the day she showed up to help with Aimee's situation."

She had him there. Those were his feelings as well.

"Love looks good on you, Son." His mother smiled. "I know, I know, you haven't said you love her yet, but I can tell."

Keith chuckled. Few people in the world truly got him. His mother was one of them.

"I had to learn to read you, ever since you were a baby. You were always so quiet, so thought-filled. Just because you weren't talking didn't mean you weren't taking in everything. You missed nothing. It's what makes you such a good soldier. You read people and situations better than anyone I've ever seen."

Keith took a deep breath and frowned. Looked out toward the horizon. It was a gorgeous day. Cool and crisp. Perfect.

"I see that frown. Don't believe for a second what happened with Mandy was all your fault."

Uncanny, how she read his mind. "I didn't read that situation or person well at all though, did I?"

She shook her head. "That was different."

"Different how?"

His mother took a deep breath in and let it out. "You were so young. Not that that's an excuse. You could read people then too. But you were so set on how you wanted life to be, I think you tried to force something that just wasn't going to settle in how you wanted."

"You never said this to me."

She shrugged. "You were young, but you were a grown man. I prayed for what I thought was best, but God had another plan."

He sure did. Keith had been trying to figure out just exactly what it was. Another first since meeting Torie—he didn't think about that anymore.

"What if I'm trying to force things with Torie to be a certain way? What if I make the same mistake again?"

"Ah, the 'what ifs' in life. Those are tough cookies." His mom nodded then looked at him, her head cocked. "But I don't see that happening with Torie. She's independent, confident, can take care of herself. I would imagine that's what you love most about her."

Yet again, his mother was dead on.

She continued. "And you're wiser now, and more realistic about what you want from life. I could see Torie supporting you no matter what."

Man, he hoped she was right there.

She patted his knee. "I'm right. We women can sense these things."

Keith chuckled.

"My intuition tells me Torie's life hasn't been so easy either. I'd be willing to bet she has some wisdom from her experiences as well that have made her cautious, and honest with herself about what she wants from life."

Keith nodded. "Her dad was…not a nice man." He'd promised Torie he wouldn't tell anyone her story. Not without her permission. His mother was a vault. She'd never share anything. But still. He was a man of his word. And his mother knew it too.

She nodded. "Got it."

"She's been carrying a lot of junk on her own. For a long time."

"And yet she's trusted you with it."

Again, not a question.

"Yes ma'am." His hat moved up and down as he nodded.

"Good. She senses in you what she should—a man she can trust."

"She's worried I'll walk away from her."

"Makes sense." His mom leaned back in her chair, wove her fingers together, and rested her hands in her lap.

"I won't."

"Of course you won't." His mother's confidence was firm, her tone gentle.

"She thinks I couldn't love someone like her. Someone not…perfect. I tried to tell her God can make her whole."

"Did she believe you?"

"I think she believes God loves her. But she just hasn't let Him heal that part of her yet."

His mom nodded. She didn't respond right away. He loved that about his mother. Like him, she thought before she spoke, wanted her words to matter.

She reached for his hand and held it. "Well, then, you two are quite good for one another, aren't you?"

"What do you mean?"

She held his gaze with hers, eyes as blue as the sky, same as his, bore into his soul. "Torie's never had a male influence in her life that allowed her to see God as loving. Forgiving. You can be that man for her, the man I raised you to be. Perfect? No. But honorable, kind, protective. Love her at all costs. And she can teach you it's okay to let God heal *your* past and move forward."

Keith closed his eyes. He lifted his mother's hand to his lips and kissed her knuckles. "I love you, Mom."

She patted his cheek. "I know you do, Son. And I love you." She pushed out of the chair and stood. "Now, we have a party to prepare for. Let's tackle those twinkle lights."

Keith laughed, his bad attitude gone. For this woman, he would do anything. Even tackle thousands of tangled twinkle lights.

As they moved around, setting up chairs and hanging decorations, Keith thought about what his mother had said. She was right. She usually was. He loved Torie. It was time to tell her. And then hope she'd let him spend the rest of their lives showing her.

15

A BELL TINKLED above the door as Torie entered the coffee shop. She'd noticed the little hole in the wall when Keith drove them through town the other night and was glad she and Rae were meeting there. It looked charming and warm and she wanted to see inside.

It sat on a corner of the main drag through town, windows all along the front and side. A long pastry counter flanked a cash register, and espresso machines and such filled the counter behind.

The scent of fresh-brewed coffee wafted through the room, filling Torie with a sense of goodness. Johnny Mathis crooned about dreaming of a white Christmas and chatter from people at tables filled the room. Little sprigs of holly berries adorned each table and poinsettias all around filled the place with Christmas cheer.

Either because they were intimidated by her or, in all honesty, because she didn't make the effort, Torie hadn't connected with too many women over the years as friends. Sure, she had people in her life who were fun to hang out with, go to a movie or whatever on the weekend. But no true friends, besides Aimee.

Rae waved to Torie from a table near the side window. A bright green snow hat sat atop her red waves. She wore a long-sleeved white sweater and red vest. Her porcelain skin dusted with freckles had to be the envy of every woman in town. Knowing it probably wouldn't sound right to say, Torie thought she looked… adorable. Cheery Christmas with a pinch of spice. She settled for a different compliment as she took off her coat, hung it on the back of the chair across from Rae, and sat down.

"You look beautiful today." The woman's cheeks glowed pink.

"Thank you, ma'am. As do you." Rae frowned. "Of course, you could be wearing nasty sweats with no makeup and your hair a rat's nest, and still turn heads."

Torie rolled her eyes.

"Sorry," Rae apologized. "You probably get that a lot."

"I won't lie. It gets old."

Rae gave an over-exaggerated sigh and placed the back of her hand against her forehead. "Oh yes, the struggle is real for so many of us."

Torie laughed. "All right. Fair enough."

Rae laughed too and patted her hand. "I'm just teasing. Let's go get some coffee and carbs." The two women stood and Rae gave her a horrified look. "Wait. You do eat carbs, don't you?"

"Can't live without 'em."

Rae put a hand to her chest and said, "Oh thank God. We can be friends then." She headed to the counter to order her coffee.

A few minutes later with coffee in hand, they sat back down and settled in, Torie with her almond croissant and Rae with a blueberry scone.

"So, how was horseback riding?"

"How did you…?"

Rae shrugged and tore off a piece of scone. "The guys talk." She popped the piece in her mouth and chewed.

Right. Keith had talked to Tony about her situation. If Tony told Rae about the horseback riding, he most likely told her about Torie's dad as well.

"It was nice, actually." Torie answered. She would keep the conversation light, see what Rae knew. But every fiber of her being was certain she could trust Rae. And Tony. "I'd never ridden before so I was nervous, but once we got going, I liked it. It's relaxing."

"That it is. Tony and I try to ride every day."

"That's nice. Do you have a ranch as well?"

Rae smiled. "No. But we'd like to someday." She got a

far-off look in her eye, one filled with a family and a future with her husband.

Torie'd never daydreamed about that herself. Until now. Until Keith.

"We need to wait until he's out of the service. For now we rent a small cabin not far from the Scotts' place, actually. Tony likes that I'm near them if I need something while he's on a mission."

"How much longer does he have in the Marine Corps?" Torie took a bite of her croissant. The flaky bread and sugar melted on her tongue.

"About a year. Same as Keith." Rae tore off another bite of scone and dunked it in her coffee.

Torie nodded, aware of how much she still didn't know about Keith. They'd spent all their time unpacking her life. "How often is he on a mission?"

"It depends." She leaned forward, her elbows on the table. "Look. I'm a pretty good judge of character and I like you. A lot. You seem like a straight shooter. I am too. So, here goes. Being with a solider like Keith or Tony isn't easy. Worth it, yes, but it takes a woman cut from a certain cloth to endure it."

"I never said Keith and I were..."

Rae held up a hand to cut her off. "Words are not necessary. I've seen how you look at each other. Fight it all you want, you're madly in love. And I adore the man like a big brother. A really big brother."

Torie laughed. Next to Keith, Rae looked like a munchkin from the *Wizard of Oz*.

"So this is why I'm telling you all of this. He's been hurt. Bad. That's why he's gun-shy with women. Thinks he doesn't deserve a happy ending. But my Lord, the man's a saint, if you ask me. If anyone deserves to be happy, it's him. And you, my friend, make him happy." She lifted her coffee mug in a toast before taking a sip.

Torie's cheeks flushed with heat. Keith made her happy too. He made her want to be the woman he needed. To be "cut from the right cloth" as Rae had described. But she needed to understand more about him. Wanted to understand more.

"He hasn't talked about his past with me. I hate to say it, but we've been attacking my demons recently."

Rae placed a hand on Torie's arm. "Yeah. Tony told me a bit about what Keith said about your dad. I hope it's ok. Not a keeper, the old man, was he?"

Torie laughed. "That's an understatement."

"Hey, I work with lots of people who have ugly pasts. If you ever want to talk, you let me know."

Torie nodded. "Thanks. I will. I'm a little talked out about it right now though. Like I said, I unloaded on Keith yesterday. Poor man."

"Don't you worry about him. He's got big shoulders. He can carry the load with you."

"Yeah. I've never had anyone to share the load.

It's...nice." She took a sip of her coffee. "So, tell me. What *is* it like to be married to a Special Forces Marine?"

Rae sat back in her chair. Her fingers wrapped around her coffee mug and she looked out the window. "It has its good and bad, just like any other marriage, I suppose." She looked at Torie and attempted a smile, but her eyes were sad. "They don't know when their next mission will be, so Tony will get a call and then have to leave with just a few days' notice. Sometimes a few hours'. I've tried to train myself to not tense every time his phone rings, but I can't." She looked out the window again. Her thumb on her left hand spun her wedding ring around as if touching it made Tony closer.

Man, to be in love like that must be something. Keith's face popped into Torie's head. Yes. She wanted that with him. Wanted to be what brought him back from each mission. The one who greeted him, welcomed him home.

"How long is he usually gone?"

Rae sighed and took another sip of coffee. "It depends. Anywhere from three to six months."

Torie missed spending just one day with Keith. She couldn't wrap her head around him being gone for months at a time. "That's a long time."

"Yes, it is. The worst part is I'm not allowed to know where he's going. I have no clue what part of the world he's in. I wait. He calls when he can. FaceTime mainly. He can't say much, though, with our conversations being monitored. Basically I just get to hear his voice, know he's alive." Tears formed on her long lashes but she swallowed hard and blinked. They didn't fall. This woman might be tiny, but she was made of tough stuff. The kind of stuff it took to be with a man like Tony. A man like Keith.

Did Torie have that kind of resolve? She thought so, but listening to Rae, she wasn't so sure. Could she handle going for God only knew how long before hearing from Keith? Worrying constantly and jumping every time the phone rang?

"I try not to watch the news. If I see something happening overseas that could potentially be him and his team and I haven't had word from him, I lose it. Fearing that infamous knock on the door isn't fun either. My friends always call before coming over when he's gone. Surprise visitors are frowned upon."

"How do you get through it?"

Rae looked her in the eye. "Prayer, my friend. Lots and lots of prayer." She took a deep breath. "And faith in my husband. He and his team are the best. They're trained and they know what they're doing. He has to know I believe in him, that I'm praying him home, confident in his abilities. I save any tears or frustration for between me and God late at night when the fear grips me." She smiled. "It can't win though. God trumps fear every time."

Torie's gram used to read the Bible to her, talk to her about God. But no one had ever said what Rae had. That God had her back no matter what. Even fear couldn't hold her. Was that true? Could it be true for Torie?

Their conversation was interrupted when two women stopped at their table. One had dark hair, the other blonde. The blonde looked at Torie and said, "So, you're the one who managed to nail down the stoic, unreachable Keith Scott."

Caught off guard, Torie just sat there.

"Felicia. So lovely to see you." Rae's tone dripped of sarcasm.

Felicia looked at Rae for a moment and said, "Hello, Rae." Her eyes moved back to Torie and looked her up and down, her mouth puckered, like she'd eaten a lemon.

Torie's brain caught up with what was happening and she recognized the woman as one of the ones vying for Keith's attention at the dance club the other night. Hmph. Two could play this game.

She stood, all six feet of her—six feet, three inches with her boots on. "It's so nice to meet you. I'm Torie." She attempted to shake the woman's hand but as expected, Felicia's eyes grew wide as Torie towered over her. She stared at Torie's hand like it was poisonous.

In a huff, the woman turned on her heel and left the coffee shop, her little brunette tagalong in tow.

Torie sat back down and sipped her coffee.

Rae's jaw dropped as she stared at Torie. "That. Was. Awesome." She laughed until tears filled her eyes.

"I mean it," Rae said when she finally caught her breath. "That was so freaking cool. The look on Felicia's face was priceless."

Torie shrugged. "Sometimes the height thing comes in handy. It's intimidating."

Rae huffed. "Oh, Chica. It was not just your height. Believe me."

"I noticed them at the club the other night. They were like Keith groupies."

"Bleh. Ignore them. They were dropped on their heads as children."

Torie laughed again. Man, she liked this woman. It was turning out to be a great day.

"Come on. Let's go shop. You need the perfect outfit for the party tomorrow night."

Torie nodded. "Let's do it."

* * *

That night, Torie snuggled down deep in the covers of her bed and sighed. It had been a perfect day. Well, as perfect as a day could be without seeing Keith. On cue, her phone rang.

Keith.

She tapped the accept button on her phone and answered. "Hey there."

"Hey yourself." His baritone voice through the phone made her shiver.

"Sorry I'm calling so late. Mom's a slave driver when it comes to parties."

The teasing tone of his voice only made it sound sexier. How was that even possible?

"It's okay. My day with Rae went from coffee to shopping to dinner. I only got home just a bit ago."

"I'm glad you had a nice day. Rae's the best."

"She is. She had some fine things to say about you too."

"Uh-oh. I forgot how you women talk. Now I'm worried."

Torie smiled. His tone didn't say worried. She could practically see him grinning on the other end of the line. Those dimples peeking through. Goodness, the man could heat her up when he wasn't even in the room.

"We women? Sounds like you and Tony chat more like girls than we women do."

He laughed. "You got me there. He's the best as well. Not anyone else I'd rather have my back, in battle and in life."

Torie's smile fell. She thought of all Rae had told her on their coffee date. There was so much to what Keith and Tony did as soldiers. Being in his life wouldn't be for the faint of heart. But her heart was too far gone to turn back now.

"Is everything ready for the party?" A positive topic sounded like a good idea. "Close. Dad and I still have some stuff to do tomorrow. You gonna be okay another day on your own?"

"I wasn't on my own today."

"True. Let me rephrase. I hate going two days without seeing you."

She smiled. "I like that phrase much better. But yes, I'll be fine. A nice down day in the cabin sounds good. I'll curl up by the fire and read." She was also going to do a little research, see if she could find anything out about her dad's whereabouts. But telling Keith that would only worry him. Get him more riled than he already was about it. No. She'd keep that to herself. If she found anything, she'd let him know.

"I'll bring Bones over in the morning if you want. I'm sure she'd love a snuggle day by the fire, if that's good with you."

"I would love that! Thanks." He was offering up the dog because of how much she loved Bones, but Torie was also aware it would make him feel better if she had a guard dog for the day. Since he couldn't be one. "Of course, I'd rather snuggle you."

Keith's voice grew dangerously low. "Believe me when I say that's exactly how I'd like to spend my day."

Her insides tingled. "From what you've said about this...project of your mother's, I believe you."

Keith blew out a long breath. "Yeah. I love this party. I do. And I love my mother. But project it most certainly is."

She giggled. Good Lord. That man had turned her into a giggler.

"Get some sleep, Dragonfly. I'll drop Bones off in the morning and then we'll dance the night away tomorrow night."

"Sounds like a plan, Captain. I'll see you tomorrow."

Torie ended the call and set her phone on the nightstand. The thought of looking for her dad didn't leave a knot in her gut like it used to. Rae had said Keith had the big shoulders to help her carry the load. And boy, that was the truth. Having Keith in her life lifted that burden in ways she never could've imagined.

With images of dancing the night away held secure by those same big shoulders, Torie drifted off to sleep.

16

TORIE PARKED HER truck amidst the rows of vehicles that made the field next to the main house look like a parking lot. Had the entire town turned out for this party? Keith said his parents threw one every year on December 23. It was a Scott tradition. But he failed to mention just how large an event it was.

She hopped out of her truck. Music floated through the air, drawing her toward the back of the house. Brad Paisley was singing about how Santa looked a lot like Daddy. She turned the corner and stopped.

The back deck was full of people talking and sipping drinks. Twinkle lights flowed above them like lightning bugs in the night sky. An enormous dance floor was set up just beyond the deck, lights covering it as well. Tables and chairs surrounded the dance floor, each table adorned with red and green tablecloths and Christmas decorations. Along one side of the deck was a table about a mile long covered with silver serving bins of food, people in line filling plates and chatting.

Festive didn't even begin to describe it. A magical wonderland was more fitting. Boy, Ellie did up Christmas and she did it up right.

Torie stood there, a wave of insecurity washing over her. She enjoyed a good party as much as the next girl, but going to a country bar where she didn't know anyone was one thing. This was different. These were Keith's friends. People who were close to the Scott family. Would she make a good impression? Would they consider her good enough for him? The moment in the coffee shop with Felicia flashed through her mind. Sure, Felicia wasn't exactly Keith's friend, Torie could handle her. But these people cared about him.

She was about to back away when she caught sight of Keith. He stood near one of the tables, talking to a man with silver hair and a black cowboy hat. Keith's hat was tan, a dressier one than he wore during the day. His deep blue collared shirt sat perfectly under his dark brown jacket. The evening was cool. As always, his jeans sat loose on his hips, a silver belt buckle shimmering in the lights.

Torie smiled. Her instinct to turn and run vanished. Keith laughed at something the man said then caught sight of her. His eyes softened and his grin deepened, the dimples making their appearance just for her. He excused himself from the conversation and headed towards her. His eyes soaked her in as he approached.

She was grateful to Rae for talking her into buying the dress she wore. It was a tan and sea-foam green pattern. Long sleeved with a v-neck and tapered waist, but her favorite part was the skirt. It went to just above her knee in front then flared out to the floor, the slit in front the perfect showcase for her favorite boots. Dark brown with cutouts of green and blue throughout. She added a chunky turquoise necklace and jean jacket for good measure, and it was hands down one of her best outfits yet. Based on the heat in Keith's eyes, he thought so as well.

He stopped right in front of her, his boots toe-to-toe with hers. Looking down into her eyes, no one else existed but the two of them.

"You take my breath away, Dragonfly."

She smiled. "You clean up mighty nice yourself, Captain."

He still hadn't touched her and yet every nerve ending in her body tingled. His eyes searched hers. He wanted to kiss her, she sensed it, but he was waiting for her permission.

Fair enough.

Leaning up on her tiptoes, she put her hands on his chest and kissed him. Soft and sweet, but most definitely for all to see. He wrapped his arms around her waist and pulled her close, deepening the kiss. Apparently he was ready for the world to know more about them. And she was happy to oblige.

When he pulled back she sighed and rested her forehead against his chest. "It feels like it's been longer than two days since I've seen you."

His chest rumbled against her head as he laughed. "I know exactly what you mean."

They'd seen each other briefly during the day when he dropped off Bones and picked her back up again. But he was moving quickly, Ellie needing him to get things ready for the party.

He lifted her face to look at him. "You're okay though?"

"Yes." He meant her dad. No news was good news, right? Keith had texted her throughout the last two days so he knew there was nothing to tell, but he'd asked anyway. Checking in on her, protecting her. Man, she never thought she'd say it but she loved it. Loved being taken care of.

Torie looked around them. People were looking their way, whispers floating through small groups. Mostly women, of course. She didn't care. "I cannot believe what you and your mom have done here. It's amazing."

Keith turned to look with her but kept one arm around her waist, her body tucked in beside his. "It does turn out nice, doesn't it?"

"You sound skeptical."

He smiled down at her. "If you had seen this place yesterday, you'd be doubtful yourself."

"Ah, the twinkle light debacle."

Keith winced. "Please don't bring that up. I've had nightmares. Trying to get it out of my mind."

Torie laughed and Keith kissed her on the top of the head. She'd never been this happy.

"Is it always like this? Outside under the stars? It's magical."

"No. We've rented a big tent most years because it's too cold or snowing. But Mom watches the weather like a hawk for weeks before. We've had unusually warm winters, so we've been able to have it outside for a few years. The heaters help." He pointed to the tall silver lanterns scattered among the crowd.

"Let's go find my parents. They'll want to say hi to you."

She nodded in agreement. He led them around the tables to the back deck where Colt and Ellie were talking with a group of people. As soon as Ellie saw Torie, she politely broke away and came over for a hug.

"Torie, dear. It's so wonderful to see you." The woman's southern drawl was smooth as honey and just as sweet. She pulled back from their hug and looked Torie up and down. "Now that dress is simply fabulous. You must tell me where you found it." With that, she hooked her arm in Torie's and led her to the drink table.

* * *

Keith watched as his mother whisked Torie away to get drinks. Man, the woman was gorgeous. When he'd caught sight of her standing there alone, that dress showcasing her mile-long legs and flowing golden hair down her back, he'd almost fallen over. He'd been talking to George Henderson about a new horse, but anything they'd been saying floated into the wind the minute Torie breezed into his sights. His instinct to be near her was so fierce, a herd of wild horses couldn't stop him.

"She's something special, isn't she, Son?" Keith had forgotten his dad beside him, his thoughts completely on the woman now shaking hands with Angie, his mom's oldest and dearest friend. Torie tucked a strand of hair behind her ear, the diamond stud glittering in the light. He frowned. He made a mental note to ask who those were from.

His dad laughed, drawing him from his thoughts.

"Oh boy, you're in further than I thought."

"What's that, Dad?"

"I could tell you had feelings for that lovely young lady the first night she came to dinner. I just didn't see until now how strong those feelings were."

"You can tell all that, huh? I need to get better at masking my thoughts."

"I'm your father. You can't fool me. And I know what love looks like."

He sure did. His dad got that goofy grin on his face every time he looked at Keith's mom. When Keith and Dane were kids they'd tease their parents, found it gross how mushy they were towards one another. But then they grew to understand exactly how special that relationship was and both desired it in their own lives. Dane had found his with Aimee. Keith had thought he found his, but was wrong. That's what his mother must have meant when she said he had an idea of what he wanted from a relationship and tried to force it.

His intentions had been good. He truly thought he had that. But he was wrong. Could he be wrong about Torie too? She threw her head back and laughed at something Angie said. Her face glowed. Relaxed and happy looked damn good on her. He had every intention of keeping things that way.

"Excuse me, Dad. I need to see a girl about a dance."

His dad tipped his cowboy hat to him and smiled. "I understand completely, Son."

Keith made his way over to the women. "I'm sorry to interrupt, ladies, but I was wondering if I might ask this lovely lady for a dance." He held his hand out to Torie, who blushed. Out of the corner of his eye he saw his mother and Angie grinning, but his focus was on the angel in front of him.

"I would love to." She took his hand and let him lead her to the dance floor. Lady Antebellum began to sing about all they wanted for Christmas as Keith moved them at a slow pace to the beat of the song.

Keith held her close, room enough for only their joined hands between them, his other arm wrapped securely around her waist. With her heeled boots on, her face was the perfect height to nuzzle into his neck. He placed a light kiss on her ear and breathed in the scent of lemons.

"Those are beautiful earrings."

"Thank you. Aimee gave them to me for my birthday last year."

Ah, God bless Aimee. No boyfriend. No ex-boyfriend he'd have to watch out for. Excellent news. He kissed her cheek and then her forehead.

"You keep kissing me and people are gonna start asking questions," she whispered in his ear. "Start rumors." His body heat went up a notch.

"Let 'em."

"You sure you're ready for that, Captain?"

He pulled back so he could look into her eyes. "I don't give a rat's backside what people have to say. All that matters is us. That we know what's happening here."

She looked down at his chest, her body moving along with his easily to the music. "And what exactly is happening here?"

He placed a finger under her chin and lifted it until her eyes met his. "I'm falling in love with you. That's what's happening."

Her eyes twinkled in the lights and she ran her teeth along her bottom lip. Good Lord, if that didn't get his heart racing, nothing would.

"I'm glad to hear that, Captain." Her voice was just above a whisper. "'Cause I'm falling pretty hard for you too."

He kissed her. Slow and steady, never missing a step to the song. When he pulled back, she smiled up at him.

"I'm happy to hear that, Dragonfly."

"Happy looks good on you."

He chuckled. "So people keep telling me."

* * *

The rest of the evening went by in a bit of a blur. Keith danced with a few of his mother's friends, but made sure Torie was always in his sights. She danced with his dad and with Tony. She sat and chatted with Rae as if they were old friends, giggling and laughing the night away. Keith couldn't remember the last time he'd felt this good. This alive. Not once had he thought about his past, any of his missions, nothing but tonight. Tonight was about family. About Torie.

His mom pulled him away for a few moments, having him carry some of the empty food bins into the kitchen. As he headed to the backyard again, he turned the corner and stopped dead in his tracks. He could see one corner of the dance floor from where he stood and what he saw made his blood run cold.

Clint had a hold of Torie's arm, trying to pull her to the dance floor. He could see she was trying to be polite in telling him no, but he wasn't listening. Of course he wasn't listening.

Keith's feet moved fast but without drawing attention. The last thing he wanted was a scene at his parents' party. He reached them and stepped in front of Clint, Torie behind him blocked almost entirely by his body. He'd be damned if that man was going to be anywhere near her ever again.

"We really gonna go through this again, Clint?"

The weasel had the nerve to look him in the eye. "I just wanna dance, man. What's the harm in that?"

"The harm is that you're drunk. And if memory serves, not invited." Keith kept his voice down but the venom was apparent. He made sure of that.

Clint waved a hand in Keith's face. "You were always such a dud, Scott. Not a partying bone in your body. No wonder Mandy didn't want…"

"It's time you leave, Clint." Keith took a step towards him, towering the man. Torie's hand wrapped around his forearm. Not to stop him, but to let him know she had his back. It made him love her even more.

"Let's go, Clint." A female voice broke in. Mandy stepped next to Clint and put her arm through his. She looked up at Keith with apologetic eyes. Keith blinked and looked down at her. Her dress was long and flowing but her belly was apparent, round like a basketball.

She pulled on Clint and he followed her, spewing expletives as he went. They walked around the side of the house and into the night.

His mother and father appeared, and Keith looked around. The only ones who seemed to notice what had happened were those right nearby, and they all nodded to

Keith and went about their talking or dancing. A scene might have been averted, but Keith's heart hammered in his chest. Not moments before he was on cloud nine, his only thoughts of a future with Torie. Then his past slammed into him like a Mack truck. He struggled to breathe.

"Are you all right, Son?" His mom's voice broke through his thoughts. "I'm so very sorry. I had no idea they'd be here. I invited Mandy's mother. We are still friends. They must have come with them not thinking…" Her voice trailed off.

"Keith." Torie stepped around from behind him. She looked concerned. For him. Man, how did everything go to crap so fast? He looked into those hazel eyes and his heart wrenched in his chest.

"Keith. Who was that? Who is Mandy?"

He looked down at Torie. There was no way around telling her. He had waited and now it crashed into him without warning.

"Mandy was my wife."

17

DID KEITH JUST say his wife?

Torie's mind spun as she watched Keith walk away from her and into his parents' house. One minute her world was magical, the next it was as if the stars were crashing down around her.

"Sweetie. You need to go talk to him." Rae put her hand on Torie's arm as she spoke. Somehow in the midst of what happened Tony and Rae had turned up by her side. A pattern of sorts, them always there to back Keith up. She looked down at Rae and then over at Tony. They were backing her now too.

She took a deep breath. "I don't know. It seems as if he'd like to be alone."

Tony shook his head. "No. You two need to talk about this."

Torie looked once again to Rae, who nodded and smiled at her. "It's all good, honey. I promise. You two can talk this one out." She nudged Torie towards the house.

Torie's head agreed but her heart stuttered. With each step she took towards the house, her brain tried to wrap around what had just happened. The quiet of the house was drastic compared to the party outside. She closed the glass doors behind her, muffling the sound.

Keith was in the great room, facing the fireplace, one hand on the mantle, his head hung low. His hat blocked his face but Torie sensed his pain. She watched him from the doorway. Such a formidable man, yet broken inside. There was so much she still didn't know about him, but what she did know was he didn't wear his heart on his sleeve. He only shared that with a precious few, and her heart warmed at the thought that she was one of them. That he'd let her in. And she understood. Boy, did she ever. Building walls to protect yourself, to protect others. They were private people, the two of them.

She thought of backing away, giving him space. That's what she would want. Well, it was what she wanted before Keith entered her life. Now, sharing things with him sounded much more appealing. But she wasn't so sure he was there yet.

"You can come in. I won't bite." His baritone voice filled

the quiet room. He lifted his head, his eyes finding hers. Goodness. She could swim in those pools of blue for days. But her heart ached at the pain that filled them.

"We've been divorced a year now."

She moved closer to him, her boots making a thud on the wood floor with each step. She stopped beside him near the fireplace. Her hands burned to reach out and touch him, comfort him in some way, but she was still unsure of what he needed. "What can I do?"

He closed his eyes and shook his head. "You're something else, you know that, Dragonfly?"

"In a good way, I hope." She smiled at him.

He smiled back. A small quirk from one side of his mouth, but a smile none the less. Small victories.

"In every good way."

He moved to the large ottomon nearby and sat down. His shoulders hunched forward with the weight of the world on them, his elbows rested on his knees.

"Mandy and I were high school sweethearts. We both grew up here, loved the small town. I thought we wanted the same things. The same kind of life."

"What happened?"

"I joined the Marine Corps. Mandy said she was okay with it at first. As soon as I could cut it I went Force Recon. The long stints of being gone were tough on her. They were tough on me too. But she wanted me to quit. Leave. And that's not…" He took his hat off and ran a hand through his hair. He put the hat back on his head.

Torie joined him on the ottoman. She needed to be near him. Needed him to know she was close. "And that's not an option. That's not you. You're a Marine. It's not something you do, it's a part of who you are."

He looked at her, his eyes narrowing. "Yeah. Exactly." He shook his head and looked down at his hands. "We grew apart. Whenever I was home, she was angry with me. Couldn't understand. We'd talked about having a big family but then she said she changed her mind. Didn't want to bring a child into the world…into our world."

The hurt in his voice ripped through Torie as if it were her own. She could only imagine how painful those words must've been for a man like Keith. Torie thought of what Rae had said at their coffee date about how Tony needed to know Rae believed in him, in his abilities. That his wife was praying him home. The broken man before her was living proof of that truth.

Torie rubbed his back but didn't say anything. Keith hadn't pushed her when she unloaded her ghosts on him. She was happy to return the favor.

"I came home after a six-month mission to find she was having an affair with Clint. Who, to add insult to injury, had been my best friend in high school."

Torie held her tongue.

"I know. I know. But he was different then. Life's been hard on him. I'm not excusing his behavior or how he's turned out, I'm just saying....things were different."

Torie had noticed Mandy's pregnant belly the minute she'd walked up to Clint. That had to be yet another painful injury for Keith. She wouldn't have a family with him, but the town troublemaker was just fine? Torie closed her eyes and took a deep breath. Everything in her wanted to punch Clint's lights out and shake Mandy for all the hurt she'd caused. But what good would it do?

She tucked her arm under Keith's and held his hand. Her head resting against his shoulder, they sat looking at the fire that crackled in the fireplace. And really, who was Torie to judge anyone? Mandy had made decisions, mistakes just like everybody else. All Torie cared about now was the man beside her. The man he was right now. At this moment, with her.

"I can't believe you haven't started running now that you know all my dark, ugly secrets."

She rubbed her thumb along the side of his hand. "Nah. I hate running."

He laughed. That all-male, deep sound from his chest that made her toes tingle and her heart warm. He kissed the top of her head. "So what now, Dragonfly?"

She sighed. "We take it one day at a time, Captain. One day at a time."

* * *

Keith watched the flames flicker in the fireplace. Torie's

thumb rubbed along his hand, sending a different kind of fire through his system. Her fingers were long and thin, graceful and feminine intertwined with his rough, calloused hands that trained horses and shot rifles. They were so different and yet, similar in so many ways.

When he'd heard Mandy's voice outside earlier, memories washed over him. Sure, they saw each other from time to time. It was a small town. But they never spoke. He'd also heard through the grapevine she was pregnant, but seeing her that way was like a punch to the gut.

Like a tidal wave crashing down on him, he'd thought his world was going to wash away with the tide. Torie would find out the truth about him and take off without looking back.

But she hadn't.

This amazing tower of strength beside him came after him and asked what she could do. For him. She only wanted to help him. How was that possible? He didn't deserve this precious gift that leaned her lemon-scented head against his shoulder, comforting him with her presence, but he was damned sure he'd do everything in his power to keep her there.

"You're thinking way too hard."

He kissed the top of her head. "I don't deserve you."

She looked up at him, those hazel depths soaking into his soul. "I was thinking the same thing about you. I guess that makes us a perfect pair."

He cradled her face in his hand and lowered his head, covering her mouth with his own. He could get lost for days in those lips, those eyes, his hands tangled in her golden locks. His own private heaven.

When he pulled back, he tucked her against him again, if only to give them both time to catch their breath. And him time to cool down. The room was heating up fast and it wasn't from the fire.

"When will you go on your next mission?"

His heart sank with her question.

"I don't know. I get a call and I go."

"Okay."

Okay? Did she just say okay?

She sat up and looked at him. "Then we face that when it comes."

"I can't ask you to do that, Torie."

"No one's asking." She turned his head to look him in the eyes. "Do you want me in your life?"

"More than you know."

"And I want you in mine. So that means we take things one day at a time and face things as they come."

It wasn't fair to ever compare Torie to Mandy, but the resolve he saw in her eyes he'd never seen before. She meant it. She would stick with him. His heart wanted so much to believe that, but his head said to wait and see how they'd do when he got the call.

A commotion outside caught their attention. They

turned to look just as his dad came through the glass doors carrying his mom in his arms.

Keith sprang to his feet. "What's wrong?"

Tony, Rae, and Angie were close behind his parents, Angie closing the doors so no one else could come in.

"Your mother's had a fainting spell," his dad said. "I'm taking her to our room."

Keith looked at his mother. Her eyes were open, but her head lay against his dad's chest, her arms wrapped around his neck. The paleness of her face stood out against his dark jacket.

Keith looked at Tony and Rae. Rae said, "The party is winding down. I'll go out and say good-bye to those who are still here. Let them know she's fine."

Angie nodded in agreement. "I'll go with you."

The two women went back outside leaving Keith, Tony, and Torie the only ones left in the great room.

"What happened?" Torie asked before Keith could. She stood beside him near the fireplace.

Tony shook his head. "She was standing next to your dad and just looked…sleepy. But then she grabbed onto his arm. He must've sensed something was wrong, because he swept her up and brought her in here."

Torie looked at Keith. "Has this happened before?"

He shook his head. "Not that I know of. She has seemed more…mellow lately, but she does get crazy busy around this time of year."

The door opened again and Angie came through with Ainsley Smith. He'd been the Scott family doctor for as long as Keith could remember.

"Angie said your mother fainted?" he asked of Keith.

"Yes sir. Dad took her to their room."

"I thought it might be a good idea if the doctor had a look at her," Angie offered.

"Thank you, Angie. That is a good idea." Keith waved the doctor to follow him. "Come with me. I'll take you to her."

He glanced back at Torie, who nodded in understanding. "I'll be right here."

Why he was still worried she'd run he had no clue. But grateful she wasn't, he led the doctor down the hall to his parents' room.

* * *

Tony went back outside to help Rae, leaving Torie alone in the great room. She looked around. The fire had died down a bit in the fireplace but still cast a cozy glow throughout the room.

Pulling her phone from her jacket pocket, she opened a game app. It looked like it was going to be a long night so why not settle in? She had zero intention of leaving until she knew Ellie was okay. She tucked herself into a corner of the sofa and started playing.

Tapping the screen, she embraced the way the game allowed her mind to zone out a bit. Her brain needed a break.

She missed getting to the next level by one move. "Darn it!"

"What? What is it?" Keith's voice boomed behind her in the empty room. He came around the sofa and plopped down next to her, his body against hers warming her. He peered over at her phone screen.

"I'm just playing a game."

"What kind of game?"

"You have to line up the pieces three in a row to score. Each level gets harder and harder. You've never heard of it?" She turned towards him, genuinely surprised.

"Nah. It sounds goofy."

She rolled her eyes. "It's a game. See." She turned her phone for him to see the screen better.

He looked at it and shook his head. "I don't trust those online things."

"You don't trust a jelly bean?" she teased.

"That's not what I said."

Of course it wasn't, but it sure was fun to crinkle that brow of his.

"How's your mom?"

"She'll be fine. She didn't completely pass out, which is a good thing. Doc is talking to Dad now. When I left she was propped up in bed telling both of them to stop fussing over her and let her go say good-bye to her party guests."

Torie smiled. She could see that scene in her mind. Her heart went out to the two men. Even with the odds in their favor, Torie's money was on Ellie.

"How did your dad take that?"

Keith chuckled. "He crossed his arms and said she'd have to go through him."

"Oh my. What did Ellie have to say to that?"

"Something to the effect of, 'That sounds appealing' but I left the room before I could hear the rest. Leave it to my parents to sound like feisty teenagers at the most inappropriate time." He turned away and looked at the fireplace.

Was he blushing? The man was blushing. He was the cutest thing Torie had ever seen. If one could ever call the gorgeous man beside her cute.

"Awww, you're embarrassed by your parents. That's so sweet."

He looked back at her then, daggers in his eyes. Well, not daggers, really. Just more blushing and a "You can stop now" kind of glare.

She laughed just as Colt came down the hall and into the room.

"She okay?" Keith asked.

Colt nodded. "She'll be fine." He shook his head and took a seat on the sofa across from them. "Doc says she's just exhausted. Worked herself too hard over this party and Christmas."

"Dad. Is there anything else going on with Mom?"

Colt looked his son in the eye. "No. There's not. She's healthy as a horse. Truly."

"This hasn't happened before."

"Never." Colt's voice was like steel. "You know your mother. She just doesn't know when to quit. We aren't in our twenties anymore but I'll be damned if she'll ever believe that. She needs to learn to take it easy."

Torie smiled as the two men talked. Colt's love for his wife was obvious, as well as his admiration for the strong woman he married. Even if he did sound frustrated. Scared was more like it. Worry for his wife was apparent in his tone and features. This was what real love looked like. For better or worse, in sickness and health. She'd never seen it before and she liked it.

She looked at Keith. Would he ever believe that she was willing to stand by him? Wait for him as he served overseas. Seeing Colt and Ellie together made her want that—a love so deep it surpassed all odds.

The doctor came into the room and gave Colt instructions. Ellie would be fine, she just needed to rest. The doctor shook Colt's hand and said, "Oh, and she's asking to see someone named Torie."

All eyes in the room turned to her. "Me?"

Keith looked at her and shrugged. "You better go. Lord only knows what will happen if you cross that woman."

Torie could've sworn Colt shivered.

Okay then. She gave Keith one last glance, tucked her phone back in her pocket, and headed down the hall.

18

TORIE TAPPED ON the door to Ellie's room.

"Come in."

The woman sounded every bit the steel magnolia she was, far from fragile. Torie opened the door and came in the room. Ellie was propped up in bed, big fluffy pillows behind her. The room was large, but welcoming. Cozy. Decorated in gold and maroon, it had a western motif like the rest of the house. The headboard of the bed actually had antlers and the base of each lamp on the nightstand was a cowboy boot. One would think it was gaudy but it wasn't. It was...well, it was Colt and Ellie.

"Please come sit and talk with me." Ellie motioned towards a chair next to her side of the bed.

Torie obeyed. Something about the woman almost demanded your respect and yet, she wasn't intimidating, just confident. Sure of her place in the world. Certainly in her world. Torie admired her and yet hardly knew her.

"I wanted to have a chat about what happened tonight," Ellie said.

Torie shook her head. "I'm not sure that's such a good idea, Ellie. The doctor said you're supposed to rest..."

Ellie cut her off with a wave of her hand. "Oh, pish posh. That doctor of mine, God love him, wants me to act as if I'm eighty years old and sit in a chair and just knit. Well, that's not gonna happen, I tell you."

Torie fully believed her and didn't argue.

Ellie continued. "I wanted to apologize."

"Apologize?" Now she was confused.

"Yes. I'm afraid I asked Mandy's mother to the party thinking it had been long enough, this mess between the families. At least she and I could still be friends. I never thought in a million years that Mandy and that...husband of hers, would join them." She wrung her hands.

Torie placed a hand over Ellie's. "There is no way this is your fault, Ellie. Clint and Mandy made the choice to come and to cause a scene. That's their issue, not yours."

The woman looked at her and smiled. "I hate to see my son hurting."

"I do too."

Those blue eyes, just like Keith's, twinkled. "I knew there was something special about you the first time we met."

Torie pulled her hand back and looked down at her lap. "I'm afraid there's not a whole lot that's special about me, Ellie."

"Look at me."

She did.

"Yes there is. My son sees it and so do I. You need to start seeing it for yourself."

Not completely convinced, Torie nodded.

"And you love my son."

It was a statement of fact, no use denying it. "Yes." Torie's heart raced in her chest. This was Keith's mother. She wanted her approval more than anyone.

"I assume he told you the whole story?"

"Yes."

"And you can live with what he carries?"

"All I can promise right now is that I'm willing to try."

Ellie smiled and nodded. "Atta girl." Tears formed on the woman's lashes but didn't fall. "The life he lives isn't easy."

Not until that moment did Torie ever think about how tough Keith's missions had to be on Ellie. Having a boyfriend or husband overseas was one thing. Having a son serving in the military was another. Different situations, both difficult.

Ellie sniffed, her tears swallowed and resolve intact. "He needs you."

"I need him too."

"I know you do."

"Did he tell you about…my past?"

"No. Keith is a man of his word. If you asked him to not share, he won't. He only mentioned your family life wasn't easy. I'm so sorry about that, Torie."

Now it was Ellie's turn to take Torie's hand. "My son is far from perfect. But he's a good man. Whatever happened in your lives before now doesn't have to keep you from moving forward together. In truth, it can make you stronger."

Torie nodded, words failing her. Ellie was right. She and Keith both carried pain from their past, but it didn't have to keep them from a future together.

"Now," Ellie continued, pulling her hand back and settling down further into the pillows, "I'm glad we girls had a chance to talk. If you wouldn't mind, would you please send my husband back in here? I may not want to act like I'm eighty, but I'm no dummy. If this is my chance to be waited on hand and foot for a day or so, I'm gonna take it." She winked at Torie, who laughed. How could she not love this woman?

She stood and nodded. "I'll send him right in."

* * *

It was Christmas Eve. Keith had to spend most of the day helping clean up from the party. Torie offered to help but he told her not to worry, to enjoy her day. She took the morning to grab a coffee in town and visit the bookstore again before it closed for the afternoon and evening. She'd also ordered something for Keith for Christmas and wanted to pick it up.

The whole town was shutting down around lunchtime and not opening again until the twenty-sixth. There were things Torie didn't miss about small towns, mostly gossip, but she did love the continued respect for family and holidays.

She bought groceries to last the next few days and all the ingredients for dinner. She was cooking for Keith, a special Christmas Eve meal. She needed to talk to him too. They both wanted to be in each other's life, but the logistics of that were weighing on her mind. Her job and life were in San Diego. He clearly belonged here. And God only knew when he'd be called to a mission.

She wanted a romantic Christmas Eve, but she was a woman who needed a plan. After her morning in town, she'd spent the afternoon trying to track down any leads on her dad's whereabouts but couldn't find anything. She wasn't sure if that was bad news or good news. Her gut said bad. And her gut was almost always right.

But she shut down those thoughts for now to focus on Keith. He'd arrived right on time and devoured every bite of Gram's famous lasagna she'd made. They sat on the sofa in the living room, enjoying a bottle of wine and the fire Keith had built for them in the fireplace.

The temperature had dropped quite a bit outside, making the warmth of the hearth that much more inviting. The reflection of the Christmas tree lights danced off the walls and Bones was passed out on the rug in front of the fire. Torie had Dane's Christmas mix playing from the iPod on the dock. Once again, Lady Antebellum sang about wanting only that special someone for Christmas.

Keith held Torie's hand in his and raised it to his lips for a soft kiss. "I think this is becoming our song."

She smiled and leaned on his shoulder. "I think you might be right."

They sat side by side facing the fire, Torie's feet propped up on the coffee table, her bright red fuzzy socks warming her toes. Keith's bulk took up a large part of the couch with Torie snuggled against him. Perfection.

"I'm not sure I've said this much in my life. Maybe not ever. But I don't think I could eat another bite of food if I tried." Keith patted his belly. Well, belly wasn't exactly the right word. She'd worked out with the man. Rock-hard abs was more like it.

Torie laughed. "After seeing you pound almost an entire pan of lasagna, I'm inclined to believe you."

"You sure know how to cook, woman."

She frowned. "Don't get your hopes up. I can make like three meals. That's it. And one of them is sandwiches."

"If you can make a good sandwich, you can make a man happy. Trust me. And don't you worry. I can grill a mean steak and keep us fed if you aren't up for cooking."

She smiled at the thought, but her heart sank with his words. His comment hit on the precise topic she wanted to cover with him tonight, but now that they were settled in, she considered changing her mind. He must've sensed her shift in mood because he turned so they were facing each other and asked, "Is there something wrong?"

She turned as well and criss-crossed her legs beneath her so she could face him. "No. Nothing's wrong. I just think we need to…talk."

"Uh-oh. That's never a good sign."

She laughed and swatted his arm. "It's not like that."

"You sure it's not the 'It's not you, it's me' speech?"

"Nope. Nothing like that." She shook her head.

"Phew. Dodged that bullet." He swiped at his brow with the back of his hand and smiled at her. Full dimples and all. Her toes tingled and her back-up plan of no talking and kissing him senseless came to mind.

But…there was still time for talking *and* kissing.

"What is going on in that pretty head of yours, Dragonfly? You're blushing like a schoolgirl."

She put her hands to her cheeks. They were warm but it wasn't from the fire.

"Nothing. Sorry. Okay. Talking now…"

Keith leaned towards her and put a hand on her leg. "I'm listening."

Oh man, those eyes of his. If the dimples didn't get her, those blue depths sure would. *Focus, Walker. Focus.*

"I just think we need to discuss the logistics of you and me."

He quirked an eyebrow but didn't say anything.

She took a deep breath and let it out. "You live here. I don't. I need to go back in a few days, and we have no clue when you'll get called away."

The reality of what she was saying sank in and he sat back again, his hand still on her leg. That was good. Because the smile was gone and she didn't like that at all.

He ran his other hand down his face and rubbed his chin. "You're right. But I'm not sure what to say. All I know is I want you as close as possible for as long as possible."

"Me too."

"And I hate the idea of you going back without us knowing where the hell your father is."

She put her hand on top of his. "I know. But I can't keep hiding, and you can't keep me locked in the tower like a damsel in distress."

He looked at her then, a devious gleam in his eye. "Locked in a tower, huh? Have you all to myself? Who says I can't do that?"

She giggled then leaned forward and kissed him. "Focus, Captain."

"Oh, I'm focusing all right." He held her face in his hand and deepened the kiss. Her brain turned to mush and heaven could only count how long they stayed locked together, his lips nibbling at hers and driving her crazy.

He pulled back and swiped his thumb over her bottom lip. "You have no idea how much I do wish I could just keep you here. Keep you safe."

She leaned her forehead to his. "And you have no idea how much I want to stay. But as much as I love your desire to protect me, I've been protecting myself for a long time."

He kissed her forehead then leaned back to look at her. "Yeah. You have. But not from this. Not from your dad."

She shrugged. "He's just another bad guy."

"No he's not. This is personal."

"Keith…"

"Don't fight me on this one, Torie. You know I'm right. How many times have you gone away for a long holiday break to a tight-knit place in the mountains? You're hiding and you know it. Have you ever hidden from anyone?"

No. She hadn't. Just her father. She could face down drug dealers and thugs but the thought of her dad coming after her was a different story. Keith was right.

She looked over at Bones, now snoring. Her mother had gotten her a dog when she was ten. A mutt of some kind with a shaggy coat that her dad deemed worthless. To Torie, it was her best friend in the world. She ran home from school every day, the dog waiting for her on the front porch. He'd followed her everywhere.

One day she came home from school and the dog wasn't on the porch. Her mother came out the front door, her tearstained face telling Torie all she needed to know. She ran to her room, buried her face in her pillow, and cried for a week straight. Her dad had taken her dog, her best friend, and had killed him for digging in the backyard. In a nasty, dirt yard.

After that, she'd made a corner of her closet into a fort of sorts, a place for her to tuck away and hide. It was easy to sense when her dad was in a mood. That was where she'd go. Bad things couldn't find her there. *He* couldn't find her there, or so she believed. It was the only place she felt safe.

"Hey." Keith held her face in his hands, drawing her eyes back to his. "Come back to me. Where'd you go?"

"You're right. I've only hidden from my dad." She blinked but no tears came. There weren't any more to shed for that man. She frowned. "I'm so sorry. It's Christmas Eve. I wanted it to be a romantic evening."

"It has been. It's been perfect." He still held her face in his hands. He gave her a tender kiss then sat back, wrapping one of her hands in his.

"I know better than anyone that perfect doesn't mean ignoring what needs to be dealt with. Far from it. I want you to talk to me. Always."

She nodded.

"And you're right. We need to figure out the best way to do long distance—for now—and how we'll handle the situation with your dad."

He said how "we'll" handle the situation. She liked that. Keith was aware she could take care of herself, but that didn't mean she had to deal with things alone.

The mood had gone way more somber than she'd intended. It was time to remedy that.

"Hey. I got you a present."

"Oh yeah?" Keith's eyes twinkled.

"Yeah. It's Christmas, remember?" She climbed off the couch and retrieved his gift from under the tree. There were only three. One for him, one for Colt and one for Ellie. Oh, and one small thing for Bones, but she'd had to hide that in her room. If the dog smelled rawhide, she'd be tearing at her present way before it was time.

Torie placed the gift in Keith's lap and sat back down next to him. "It's not a big deal. Just something I thought of after we ran into each other at the bookstore."

He looked at her. "You thought of a gift for me then?"

She shrugged. "Sure. I was spending Christmas here and we were friends."

"Were." He leaned forward and kissed her again. "Now, it's more."

"Much more. Open your present!"

"Okay." His large hands ripped the paper away, revealing a book.

"It's a first edition Louis L'Amour."

He looked at her then back at the book in his lap. "No way. Really?"

"I don't know the ones you already have so this may be a duplicate, but I thought it might be fun to have a first edition on your shelf."

He ran a hand over the cover as if holding something precious. "This...this is perfect. Thank you."

His kiss that time was much longer and was the best thank-you she'd ever received in her lifetime. It made her want to give him a present every day. Or at least work towards a good thank-you as often as possible.

"And I have a gift for you too," Keith said once his bone-melting show of gratitude was over. "But you have to wait until tomorrow for it." He winked.

This was turning out to be the best Christmas ever.

19

KEITH STOMPED HIS boots at the entrance to the barn. At least a foot of snow had fallen through the night, making for a winter wonderland when he woke up.

Perfect.

He couldn't have called in a better favor to God if he'd tried. He had a special morning planned for Torie and snow was a huge part of it. A back-up plan was in place if the forecast had been wrong, which it was quite a bit of the time, but God answered his prayers and a white Christmas was delivered.

As he prepped things for his big surprise, his thoughts wandered to the night before. An all but perfect Christmas

Eve. Hell, as long as Torie was with him, any day or night was perfect.

As much as he hated to admit it though, she was right. They had some logistics to work through. That was for sure. And he had more questions than answers at the moment.

As he moved around the horses, he looked up to the sky. Snow fell in soft tufts, like small bits of cotton. Yeah, they had some stuff to figure out, but nothing was going to ruin what little time left they had together right now. He'd make damn sure of that. If God was up for delivering them a white Christmas, Keith was all for making it the best one Torie'd ever had.

* * *

Keith had said to dress warm but wouldn't say why. Curiosity tugged at her as she finished pulling her hair into a high ponytail. Maybe they were going horseback riding again. She wore jeans and her old cowgirl boots just in case. A long-sleeved T-shirt with a sweater and her big jacket should be good.

She turned off the light in the bathroom. Drawn to the scenery outside, she sat on the bench in the picture window of the guest room. Quite a bit of snow had fallen overnight, turning the trees and area around the cabin into a winter wonderland. It was as if a white Christmas was delivered just for her. There was something almost magical about this place. It drew her in then wrapped her up like a warm blanket.

When she'd arrived not long ago, everything that mattered to her was in San Diego. Her work, her friends. In just a short time, so much had changed. Her intent was to be here for a few weeks to figure out what steps to take with her dad. She had no clue what was in store for her. With Keith in her life now and this place practically calling to her, she was more confused than ever. Or was she?

Aimee would be here now too. Could she leave San Diego and live here? Is that even what Keith wanted? They'd only been together a short time. Her head said it was crazy to even consider such things yet. Her heart said it might be time to take a chance and go for it.

She sighed and leaned against the window, her arms wrapped around her knees that were tucked up against her. She missed the snow. Having seasons. It was so beautiful. A palette of white with green and brown sprinkled in. No matter what happened, she would always have this time with Keith. Nothing could ever take that away.

A sound in the distance made her sit up and cock her head to listen. Were those bells? They were getting louder, but as she scanned the property she couldn't see anything. Kneeling on the window bench now, she looked through the trees. What in the world?

Her heart pounded in her chest as the scene unfolded in front of her. It was straight out of a movie. Coming up the road that led to the cabin was a horse-drawn sleigh, Keith holding the reins and Bones sitting beside him, her ears perked and a big doggie grin on her face.

"No way!" The warmth of Torie's breath steamed up the window. She rubbed it away with her hand and looked again. Nope. It wasn't a figment of her imagination. The man of her dreams was pulling up to her front door in a bright red sleigh on Christmas morning.

Like a child, she climbed out of the window seat and ran for the stairs. She opened the front door and stopped on the porch just as Keith was pulling the horses to a stop.

He jumped down from the sleigh and with his arms out wide said, "Merry Christmas." His cowboy hat and coat were dusted with snow. His blue eyes glimmered and she had to pinch herself as a reminder she wasn't dreaming. This amazing hunk of a man was here for her.

Without hesitation, she ran for him and jumped into his open arms. He caught her without faltering and held her. She clung to him, her arms and legs wrapped around him tight. His breath was warm against her neck. "So… I guess you like my present."

She pulled back and held his face in her hands. Leaning in, she kissed him, his lips cool against hers. After thanking him thoroughly, she leaned her forehead against his, her body still enveloped in his arms.

"I will take that as a definite yes."

"Yes! I love it."

He set her on her feet but kept his arms wrapped around her. "Go grab your coat. Your chariot awaits, my lady."

Torie kissed his cheek and turned to go back into the house. After putting on her coat and tucking her phone in her pocket, she locked the door. Keith held out a hand for her and helped her into the sleigh. Bones gave her a big kiss and snuggled next to her as Keith climbed in and took the reins.

"There's a blanket there next to Bones if you get cold. You can wrap up in that."

"Thanks." She scooted as close to him as she could. "I think I'll keep warm this way for now though, if that's okay with you."

He graced her with a dimpled smile. "You read my mind."

With a flick of his wrist, the reins snapped and the horses ambled forward. Torie leaned against Keith's shoulder and sighed. Bells were attached to the side of the sleigh, their jingle echoing through the trees. The clomp of the horses' hooves mixed with the slush of the sleigh gliding through the snow became a symphony that filled her ears. One of peace and joy—all the things Christmas should be.

She didn't get many presents at Christmas growing up. And Keith could've lavished gifts upon her if he'd wanted to, trying to make up for that. But instead, he put together the most romantic moment of Torie's life. Simple. Thoughtful. Generous. Just like the man sitting beside her. It was as if he gave her a piece of himself. No present would ever come close to matching it. Ever.

They rode in quiet, both soaking in the moment. One she'd never forget. Torie had never been with anyone where silence wasn't awkward. But Keith. Keith's presence had become her calm. Steady. Sure. He didn't waver. Solid on every level. And times like this brought her a peace she'd never experienced before.

They rounded a bend and emerged from a patch of trees to a clearing. Keith's cabin came into view, a mountain haven amidst the white blanket of snow. He guided the sleigh up to the front porch and stopped.

"Okay. Part two of this Christmas morning awaits."

He hopped down and came around to help her out of the sleigh. She took his hand and followed him inside, Bones tagging along behind. He opened the front door and led her inside. The warmth enveloped her right away, a welcome respite from the chill outside.

He took her coat and hung it on a rack just inside the front door. A stairway was straight ahead with a family room to the left and a dining room to the right. "Make yourself at home." He gestured to the family room. "I'm going to cook us up some breakfast."

She quirked an eyebrow at him.

"Don't look so surprised. I've been feeding myself for years. Trust me." His eyes twinkled as he kissed her cheek. "Look around while I head to the kitchen."

"Okay." Bones trotted towards the family room as Keith disappeared through the dining room. Torie decided to follow Bones. Keith said to look around and she had to admit, she was curious.

The one word that came to Torie's mind as she stepped into the family room was "grand." Everything about the place was large. Huge logs criss-crossed to make a pattern along the ceiling. The walls were made of the same type of logs standing together side by side. A fire crackled in the stone fireplace, the hearth reminding her of a historical fiction novel she'd read about Scottish warriors in the 1500s.

Keith stepped into the room, a physical reminder of why the place was grand. A man his size needed a place that could hold him. But like the man himself, it wasn't off-putting but rather, warm. Safe.

"You okay? I got coffee going. Now I just need to know if you'd like waffles or an omelet."

He looked like a kid on…well, Christmas. "Waffles sound amazing. You can make waffles?"

"I'm a man of many talents." He winked and left the room.

Torie fanned her face with her hand. Of that, she had no doubt. Cupboards opened and closed and the scent of coffee wafted into the room. Heaven. She was in heaven.

A Christmas tree sat in the corner, lit up and twinkling cheer throughout the room. Presents sat beneath, the entire picture something from a postcard or Norman Rockwell painting.

She pinched herself once more just to be sure. Nope. Not dreaming. She was here. With Keith. On Christmas.

Bones trotted into the kitchen, the potential for scraps calling as Keith moved around making breakfast. Torie followed. There was an island in the center of the room with two barstools tucked up against it. Keith stood on the other side, moving between the island and the kitchen sink that sat opposite.

He filled a mug of coffee and set it down in front of a barstool then continued with his work. She sat in front of it and took a sip. Hmmmm, just as she liked it. She watched as he set up a waffle iron and plugged it in. He tossed a dishtowel over one shoulder and whipped a whisk around a bowlful of batter. His muscles flexed beneath his dark blue Henley as he worked. Yep. It was true. This man was dropped straight from heaven just for her.

"Well, what do you think?"

For a second she thought he'd caught her staring and meant what she thought of him and his muscles. She could feel her cheeks flush so she sipped her coffee again to hide.

"Of the house," he continued.

The house. Right.

"It's beautiful. It suits you."

He stopped and looked at her. "I'm not sure what that means."

"It's a good thing. It's...big and yet, homey. Warm."

He went back to whisking, a dimple peeking out with his grin. "Ah. Got it. Well, I'm a big guy. I wanted to build something that...fit me."

"It's perfect."

A muffled ring from the hallway made them both turn and look. "Oh. Shoot. I put my phone in my coat pocket and forgot to turn off the ringer. Sorry."

"Don't be sorry."

"That must be Aimee. She's the only one who checks in on me at Christmas. Even when on her honeymoon." She rolled her eyes. "You mind if I say hi to her real quick?"

"Not at all."

Torie stood and found her way to the front door via the main hallway. By the time she got there the phone had stopped ringing. She pulled it from the side pocket and looked at the screen. One missed call and one voice mail. Without checking the number she hit play on the voice mail. Smiling, she waited to hear her friend's cheery voice through the phone line. What she heard instead made her drop to her knees in the hallway and grip her stomach.

His voice slithered through the phone like a snake. "Hey, little girl. What are you thinking, trying to hide from me? All this time and you still don't wanna see your old man? Well, you can run, baby, but you can't hide."

Torie clutched the phone in her hand as the message ended. She turned and sat with her back against the wall, her knees pulled up against her. Panic flowed through her in waves. Her breath came in spurts as tears began to run down her cheeks. He'd found her. Her phone hit the wood floor with a thud as she dropped it and buried her face in her hands.

* * *

The hair on Keith's neck stood on end when he heard the thud in the hallway. Something was wrong. He abandoned their meal and in just a few steps made it to the front hallway. Torie sat curled up in a ball against the wall, her face in her hands, her phone discarded beside her.

She sounded as if she'd just run a marathon. He sat beside her and pulled her into his lap. He wasn't a stranger to panic attacks. Her body wracked with sobs but she leaned into him, gripping his shirt and holding on as if he was her only lifeline. That was fine by him. He'd hold her forever if need be.

With one arm holding her secure against him, he stroked her hair. Some strands had come loose from her ponytail. He brushed them back out of her face and let her cry. Gave her time to catch her breath. Kissed her forehead until her breathing began to sound normal.

"What helps chase away the darkness?"

Her head rested against his chest, her hands still holding onto his shirt but not as tight. She took a few deep breaths, the weepy hiccups breaking his heart. Man, he loved this woman.

When she spoke her voice was frail. "When I was a girl, Gram would sing hymns to me as I fell asleep. I usually sing those in my head and for whatever reason, it helps."

She curled up tighter in his arms, needing to be closer. He wrapped her up and kissed her forehead. "There's a reason, alright, Dragonfly. There's a reason."

And right there on the floor of his front hallway, he hummed "Amazing Grace," the woman in his arms weaving her way into his heart and changing him forever.

20

TORIE LOUNGED ON the sofa, a mug of hot tea in her hand. A blanket was tucked around her and Bones lay on the floor in front of her. Drawers opened and closed in the kitchen, the sounds of Keith cleaning up their breakfast floating into the room.

He'd stayed with her last night. Being the true gentleman he was, he'd slept on the couch. After she'd calmed down enough to tell him what happened, what had set off her panic attack, he didn't want to leave her alone. And quite frankly, she didn't want to be alone.

She hadn't had a panic attack in years. Not as an adult, anyway. They scared the hell out of her. If it weren't for Keith, who knows where she'd be? She thought of yesterday morning. It was so perfect. Such a beautiful Christmas. But then her dad's voice in her ears sent her reeling. All those horrible memories flooding back, taking her places she vowed never to go again.

And Keith. He'd held her and comforted her unlike anyone ever had. When he'd begun humming, his chest rumbled with the sound, calming her and quieting her trembling. What man did such a thing? Held a hysterical woman in the middle of the floor and hummed to her because that chased away her darkness?

The man moving around the kitchen, that's who. The man who'd stepped into her life and shown her what it meant to be loved. Really loved.

She set her tea on the coffee table and pulled the blanket up tighter to her chin. The loss of control that came with a panic attack bothered her to no end. So much of her childhood was about someone else closing in on her and taking over.

Becoming a cop had helped her lose that feeling of helplessness, the physical and mental training for it about control and grace under pressure. But Keith was right. Things with her dad were different than what she faced each day at her job. It was personal.

Memories she had stamped down for years popped to the surface like a creepy Jack-In-The-Box and she couldn't slam the thing back down and close the lid.

The kitchen door opened and closed and muffled voices filled the kitchen. Keith had suggested Rae come over and talk to her. The old Torie would've somehow played down yesterday's episode, but the old Torie also wouldn't have had an attack in front of anyone. She'd let her guard down with Keith. Trusting him had opened her heart in a new way. She trusted Rae as well. And he convinced her that talking to Rae would help.

Rae came in the room and gave her a hug. She patted Bones on the head before sitting on the other end of the sofa from Torie. Torie could feel the warmth of Rae's hand through the blanket as she set it on her foot. A connection. A gesture of friendship that said she was there.

"Are you one of those counselors that just waits for your client to talk first?"

Rae laughed. "You've met me, girlfriend. You know I've made talking an art form. Quiet is not my specialty."

"Boy, isn't that the truth," came from the kitchen doorway. Keith stood there, drying his hands on a dishtowel.

"You hush yourself now, Hulk. And stay in the kitchen where you belong." Rae waved a hand his direction as she spoke.

That earned her a deep chuckle from Keith. "Yes ma'am. I'll just get back to my chores." He winked at Torie then waited for her smile in return before going back into the kitchen.

"He loves you something fierce, you know that?"

"I'm beginning to." Torie moved and put her legs along the sofa, her feet now right near Rae's side.

"I've been around him for a while now and let me just say, he's never looked at anyone, ever, the way he looks at you."

Torie's insides warmed at her friend's words. Sure, she could see it in Keith's eyes, but to have someone who'd known him a while say it made it that much more real.

"He also sounded beyond concerned when he called me. You gave him quite a scare."

"I know. I didn't mean to."

"Of course you didn't."

Torie sighed and took a sip of her tea. She placed the mug back down and looked at her friend.

"How much did he tell you?"

"Just that you'd had a panic attack. Said he'd leave the details up to you."

Torie shook her head. He really was a vault, not telling anyone anything without her permission. Reason number 412 she could trust the man.

"And I only need to know the details you want to tell me."

And yet another reason she could trust Rae. She took a deep breath and let it out, leaned against the back of the couch. Having told Keith her whole story gave her the courage to do it again. She poured out the details of her past to Rae, who listened without interruption.

A small part of Torie was sad to be sharing all of this with anyone before telling Aimee, but as she talked, her heart healed a bit more. Letting others in instead of shutting them out was the salve her wounded heart needed all along. She'd talk to Aimee when she returned from her honeymoon. It would be fine. Aimee had always been in her corner. Caring for her, loving her. No questions asked.

Torie finished her story. Tears had fallen as she spoke but not the sobs that had wracked her when she'd first unloaded it all on Keith. Her broken heart was scarred, but mending.

A few minutes passed before Rae said anything. "Oh my. I'm not gonna lie. I wasn't expecting anything like that."

Torie nodded.

"You are so tremendously brave."

What? Brave? How could Rae say that? She was terrified. One message from her dad and she was a quivering child again, wanting nothing more than to crawl in that corner of her closet and pray to never be found again. There was nothing brave about that.

"I mean it, Torie," Rae continued. "You've put up with a lot of crap in your life and here you are, successful in your work, fighting for others who can't fight for themselves. Putting yourself between others and harm's way, protecting them. And now you're trusting us enough to let us carry this with you. That's bravery, sweetie. It really is."

Torie shook her head. "I have no idea how you're seeing that."

"Because you didn't let your dad win. He tried to break you, but he failed."

Tears wandered to the edge of her lashes, threatening to fall. "No. I'm broken. That's for sure."

"Oh, we're all broken in one form or another. There's no way around that. But because of your gram and Aimee and Keith—people who have shown you what true love that cast out fear looks like—you've not only survived, you've prevailed."

Torie thought about Rae's words for a moment. Those people in her life *did* love her as is, brokenness and all.

Rae continued. "Your dad took things from you that he never had a right to take. But in your pain and times of fear, you've moved forward. That takes courage."

The sound of Keith's baritone humming came from the kitchen. Rae giggled. "He is just too precious, isn't he?"

Precious was a word Torie would use for a puppy, not the man that moved around the other room humming a song by The Supremes. But as she listened, precious did somehow fit.

"He carries a lot too, Torie. Stuff I don't think he's even told you about yet. He will. I know he will. But those boys come home with a lot of…memories. Things they've seen that they just as soon forget but can't. But I'm glad he found you. Lean on God, lean on him. You two will be stronger for it."

That thought brought a peace Torie couldn't explain, but she still had her doubts about their future. What would that look like?

"I'm not sure what comes next."

"I wish I had to answer for you, sweetie. You and Keith need to figure that out together. But know this, you have whatever you need to face your dad. You do. Physically and emotionally. You're not a little girl anymore. You're a grown woman who can stand up to him. Remember that."

She pointed her thumb over her shoulder towards the kitchen. "And you've got that huge lug in there to back you up. I don't know about you, but that would give me peace of mind something fierce."

Torie laughed. Rae was right. She wasn't a kid anymore. No longer the little girl that ran to the neighbors for help that fateful night, she could do this. She could face whatever was to come.

* * *

Keith sat at the kitchen table nursing his third cup of coffee. He could hear the women talking in the other room but couldn't make out what they were saying exactly.

He was no stranger to panic, waking in the night with sweat running down his face and chest over a nightmare. But to see Torie struggle for breath, to hold her while fear gripped her, terrified him. Not a man who liked being out of control, there was nothing he could do for her but hold her. Be there with her while she waded through the storm.

But what about when he couldn't be there? He still had one more year in the Marine Corps, another year of missions. Could he and Torie get through that? He tried to push down the insecurities that crept in from his past, but he couldn't.

The thought of Torie returning to San Diego alone tore at his gut. Her father would find her, Keith didn't doubt that. And yes, Torie could handle herself on a lot of levels, but with her dad? Keith gripped his coffee mug tighter.

He snapped from his thoughts when Torie and Rae entered the kitchen. They were both laughing, a sign that calling Rae was a good idea.

"Hey, Hulk." Rae leaned over and hugged him. "I gotta go, but thanks for calling me. You take good care of her, okay?" She smiled at Torie then at him.

"Will do."

She disappeared through the kitchen door and was gone.

Torie sat across from him at the table, a blanket wrapped around her shoulders, Bones faithfully sitting beside her, sniffing the air for signs of food items that might be worth begging for. Unfortunately for the dog, Keith's coffee mug was all that sat on the table.

He rose and fixed Torie a cup then set it in front of her.

"Thank you. The tea was lovely, but something stronger sounds great." She lifted the mug to her nose and breathed in before taking a small sip.

"You okay?"

"Yeah. Talking to Rae helped. A lot. Thank you for calling her."

He'd initially called Rae in somewhat of a panic himself, a tad worried Torie wouldn't be thrilled he did so without asking her. Relief flooded him now. Some color had returned to her cheeks and her eyes weren't as sad. Yes, it had been a good idea.

"She's helped me through a lot. I thought she'd be a good listening ear."

"I'm glad you have such good friends."

"They're your friends now, too." He winked. "When Tony and I came back from our first tour, we had some…baggage to carry from it. He found Rae's support group at his church and went to a few meetings. He convinced me to join him. I teased him at first. Said he was only going because he had a crush on the tiny redhead that led the group, but he was right. Being there helps chase some of the darkness away."

Torie reached across the table and took his hand in hers. "I'm so sorry."

He shrugged. "It's part of the deal. I knew that going in. Nothing can prepare you for the reality of it though. That's why Tony and I like to talk to and work with guys who are just starting out in the service. Walk them through some of what they see and do."

She sat back in her chair again and took a sip of coffee. "Can I ask you a question?"

"Shoot."

"Is that why you have to have a light on when you sleep?"

He narrowed his eyes. How did she...?

"I got up in the night and came downstairs. You'd left the kitchen light on so I turned it off. When I got up this morning, it was on again."

He nodded. "Busted." Man, he hated how that made him feel like a child.

"Hey." Torie looked him, her hazel eyes boring into his. "I didn't mean to embarrass you. How about I tell you something embarrassing to level the playing field?"

He chuckled. "Okay."

"When I was a girl, I had a corner of my closet I would climb into when I needed to shut out the world." She blinked and looked out the window. "I still do. Thankfully, my closet's a lot bigger now so there's room for a grown woman curled up in the corner but..."

Keith's heart ached for her. That wasn't embarrassing. It was gut wrenching.

She'd tried to play it off as if her curling up in the dark wasn't some big deal, but it was.

"Torie..."

She cut him off. "Hey. It's okay. Really. Like you said, sometimes we have to do things to chase away the darkness. And it goes away. It does."

He nodded.

"Keith, we need to face the fact that I have to go back. I've decided to leave the day after tomorrow."

His teeth clenched and he swallowed hard. He'd known all along she couldn't stay. They had to face reality. But having it staring him in the face wasn't something he could prepare for.

"Why so soon?"

"Because I can't keep running, keep hiding. Rae reminded me that I have it in me to face whatever happens with my dad. I'm a cop, for crying out loud. I could chase *him* down and put his butt back in jail. But I'm trapped by fear if I don't do something. And I have my friends on the force. I have backup. I'm not afraid to tell my story anymore."

He understood. Man, he understood. But he didn't have to like it. "How do you think your dad got your number?"

"I honestly don't know. But I can't imagine how he could track me just from that. He's smart, but not that smart."

"He was smart enough to get your number."

"True. I'm thinking if I go back, use my resources at work, I'll be in a position to find him before he finds me."

"Then I'm going with you." He crossed his arms and stared her down, waiting for her to protest.

She smiled. "Okay."

Wait. What? What happened to the woman who'd stood toe-to-toe with him just months before when she went in guns a-blazing to rescue Aimee, telling him he had to stay behind?

"You can wipe that look off your face, Captain." She laughed. "You've taught me it's okay to not do everything alone."

"We leave the day after tomorrow then."

"Yep."

"Well, we best make the most of the time we have left here then, don't you think?"

The twinkle in her eye said she agreed, as did the smirk she tossed his way from behind her coffee mug. "Whatever you say, Captain."

21

THE MORNING AIR was cool and crisp. Snow still covered the ground and some tree limbs, but the sun was shining and the sky was a shade of blue only God could create. Keith's favorite kind of day. Nothing like the sun on his back and the cool air against his face.

Too bad his stomach was in so many knots he wasn't able to enjoy it. He yanked on Caliber's saddle straps, tightening the girth. Torie would be there any minute. They'd decided the best way to spend their last day at the 4S Ranch was to go horseback riding.

He heard before he saw Torie's truck bouncing along the dirt road towards the barn. Why she loved that old beater he would never understand. Maybe she'd let him buy her a newer version sometime soon. Probably not. Stubborn woman. He smiled, in spite of himself.

She hopped out of the truck and walked toward him, a big smile on her face, her hair blowing in the breeze. Good Lord, she'd be the end of him. He decided then to wait and talk to her later, not ruin their day together. Keep that smile on her face for as long as he possibly could.

His heart sank in his chest when she hugged him and reached up for a kiss. "Good morning, Captain. Are we ready to ride?"

"Yes ma'am. Patsy's all ready for you."

"Great!" She sauntered over to Patsy and rubbed the horse's nose. She looked back at him, her eyes shining in the sunlight, full of joy. And his heart broke into pieces.

* * *

Torie placed her shampoo and conditioner into a plastic bag. She grabbed the few bottles of makeup and hair products from the bathroom counter and tossed those in as well before closing it.

She wanted to get an early start the next morning. San Diego was a full day's drive from Tahoe and the sooner she got on the road, the better. She sang along with The Supremes as she packed, happy about the day she'd spent with Keith and the fact that he was going with her. He could only stay a few days, but she'd take any time she could get.

He'd been unusually quiet on their ride. Not that the man was a chatty Cathy or anything, but something was bothering him, she could tell. He was coming over for dinner soon. Maybe she could get out of him what was wrong.

As if on cue, she heard the front door open and Bones's nails clicking on the wood floor. The thud of Keith's boots echoed up the stairs. She checked her hair in the mirror then headed down to greet him.

At the bottom of the stairs, she stopped. He stood by the mantle, staring into the fireplace. His hands were dug deep in his jean pockets, his brow furrowed. Something was definitely on his mind. Their trip? Was he worried about facing her dad? No, that couldn't be it. The man was Force Recon, for heaven's sake.

She went to him and wrapped her arms around his waist, leaning her head against his chest. He returned her embrace, holding her close.

"Hey you. You wanna talk about it?"

"No. Not really."

She laughed. Leave it to Keith to say it like it is.

"But we have to."

She pulled away so she could look at him. "Okay. Let's talk."

Their attention was diverted when the kitchen door creaked. Bones growled but then wagged her tail and trotted toward the kitchen.

"Helloooo? Anyone home?"

"Aimee!!!!" Torie untangled herself from Keith's embrace and bounded into the kitchen. She wrapped her friend up in her arms and squeezed.

"Now that's a greeting." Aimee's voice was muffled against Torie's torso.

She laughed and let go of her friend. "What are you doing here?" Dane stood behind Aimee just inside the doorway. "You guys aren't due home for a few more days."

Dane looked over Torie's head at Keith, now standing right behind her. The brothers exchanged a look. One that Torie didn't like.

Keith reached around her and shook his brother's hand. "Welcome home."

Dane nodded. "It's good to be home."

"Honeymoon was rough on ya, huh?" Keith teased.

"Oh, give me a hug you big oaf," Aimee said as she moved around Torie and grabbed Keith. He leaned down to hug her. She looked like a small child in his massive arms.

"Let's all go in the other room where there's more space," Aimee said after stepping out of Keith's arms. "With you two boys in here it's as if this kitchen is in a dollhouse."

They moved into the living room, Bones nudging Aimee for some attention. "Oh, you sweet baby. I missed you too." She sat on the sofa so she was face to face with the dog. Bones panted blissfully as Aimee scratched her ears.

Torie sat beside her friend on the sofa. The men stayed standing. She'd seen them together before, of course, but she now noticed the similarities. Although shorter, Dane's build was much like Keith's. Broad shouldered with a lean waist and long, jean-clad legs. However, Dane looked like his father where Keith's features were more like Ellie's.

"So… what brings you home so early?" Torie asked. "Not that I'm unhappy about it—this means I get to see you before I leave tomorrow…"

Aimee looked at Keith, her eyes searching for help.

Okay, something was going on and Torie didn't like the knot in her gut.

Keith had acted funny all day and now Dane and Aimee were home early. She wracked her brain to think of what it could be.

"Is it Ellie? Did she have another fainting spell?"

Now it was Dane's turn to look concerned. "Fainting spell? What are you talking about, Torie?"

Keith stepped towards her but looked at Dane. "Mom's fine, Dane. She got exhausted over planning the Christmas party, but she's fine." He turned his attention again to Torie. "Torie, I'm sorry. I should've just told you this morning but I didn't want to ruin our day together."

Her palms started to sweat. "What is it?"

Keith knelt in front of her and took her hands in his. "Baby, I got a call late last night. I have to leave tomorrow morning."

"Your next mission?"

"Yeah. I have to leave. And I can't go with you to San Diego."

She took a deep breath in and let it out. This? This was what he was so worried about telling her?

Taking his face in her hands, she kissed him. "Okay."

Keith blinked. "Okay?"

She smiled. "Yeah. Okay. We knew this was coming. Right?"

"Well, yeah, but…"

"But what? You need to know something, Captain. I'm not a feather that will float away when the wind blows. You got that?"

He smiled and placed his hands over hers. "Yes ma'am."

"Holy crap. Have we been gone that long?" Dane looked at Aimee, his eyes wide.

Aimee sat on the couch near Torie, her eyes glistening with tears. "Oh, be quiet and let them have their moment."

"And Captain? Why are you calling him Captain?" Dane addressed the question to Torie, ignoring his wife.

Keith and Torie laughed. "So, did you call these two yahoos home early because you thought I couldn't handle this big news of yours?"

Keith shook his head and stood. He kept a firm grip of Torie's hand. "No. I called Dane to let him know I was leaving but…"

"And we decided to come home," Aimee finished. "We wanted to see Keith before he left and I wanted to make sure you were okay going back to San Diego alone."

Torie looked at Keith. She'd be lying if she said she wasn't still afraid of her dad on some levels. But that was the child in her. Like Rae said, the woman in her was courageous, brave. She could stand up to her dad and be the support Keith needed while he was gone.

And besides, she had her friends now to help her. Rae to encourage her while Tony and Keith were gone, Aimee to care about her like she always did.

"Wait!" Torie turned to her friend. "Aimee, I'm so sorry. All this time we've been such good friends and I've never told you about me. About my past. Believe me when I say that it has nothing to do with you and everything to do with my habit of protecting myself."

Aimee hugged her. "Don't you dare apologize."

Keith cut in. "Torie. I'm sorry. I told them about your dad. When I got the call to leave, I didn't want you facing this without them knowing. I'm sorry if I betrayed your trust."

"It's fine, Keith. Really. You have my best interest at heart."

"Always."

He grabbed her hand again.

Dane shook his head then ran a hand down his face. "Wow. This is a lot to take in the first few minutes of being home."

Aimee stood and went over to her husband, wrapping an arm around his waist. "It's okay, honey. I'll explain it to you later." She patted his chest. "Now, why don't you boys go get our bags out of the truck while we girls have some talk time. Then we'll have dinner."

* * *

Aimee stood at the sink, peeling potatoes, a red apron wrapped around her.

"It's so good to see you." Torie sat at the table slicing carrots.

Aimee stopped and turned to her. "It's good to see you too." She dumped the peels in the trashcan, wiped her hands, and sat across from Torie at the table.

"I really am sorry I didn't tell you about my dad. About my past."

"I knew enough. You'd given hints over time. I didn't need details."

Torie smiled at her friend.

"So, do I get points for calling it?"

"Calling what?"

Aimee raised an eyebrow. "You and Keith. I sensed some sparks between the two of you months ago, but girlfriend, ya'll are a full-on forest fire now."

Torie laughed.

"Ah, yet another difference. You protested before but now, nothing. Even more proof that I'm right."

"Fine. You win. You called it." Torie scooped the carrots off the cutting board and placed them in a pot.

Aimee leaned her chin on her hand. "You sure you're okay with it?"

"Okay with what?"

"Him being gone? I imagine it's not easy. Dane told me about all Keith has been through. I know you're tough enough to deal. But are you ready to throw your heart in full throttle?"

Torie didn't hesitate. "Yeah. I am. I love him, Aimee. Who he is, what he does. All of it. The whole package."

Aimee wriggled her eyebrows. "He is a lovely package isn't he?"

Torie threw a piece of carrot at her friend's head. Aimee squinted as the carrot bopped her in the forehead then fell to the table.

"Hey! What was that for?"

Torie just shook her head and kept chopping.

"What about your dad? I'm worried about you going back to San Diego alone. Hey! I know! Dane and I can go with you. He can go all cop mode again and help you out."

"Cop mode? Really, Aimee. As much as I love the offer, you and Dane have a life now. Here."

"But you're my best friend. And almost family." She winked.

"Don't put the cart before the horse, girlfriend. Keith and I are taking this one day at a time."

Aimee waved her hand. "Bah. I say this time next year I'll be helping you pick out a dress."

Torie liked that idea. She liked that idea a lot. But she understood Keith being gun-shy about marrying again. They needed to wait and see what the next year or so would bring, how they handled him being gone.

"And I'll let you in on a little secret." Aimee leaned forward and whispered as if the guys in the living room could hear her. "Dane has been talking to the police here. They've got an investigative team and want him to join. I bet they could use someone with your expertise as well."

"Again, cart before the horse."

Aimee shrugged. "I'm just sayin…"

Torie knew exactly what her friend was saying. And her interest was piqued, that was for sure. The thought of living in the country again, being near Aimee and Rae was great. But she couldn't start jumping on the idea of moving up here, changing her life, before she even knew if that was something Keith wanted.

"We'll see."

"Okay. But I'm praying for you, girlfriend. God's got you, you know."

She did know. In some way, she'd always known. But had chosen to push it down, not think about it. Not anymore. She believed God loved her. As is.

Aimee stood and went back to prepping the potatoes. Torie continued her job of chopping carrots, her mind on all Aimee had said. She wasn't the type to fantasize about a white picket fence with a dog in the yard, but now Keith's cabin with Bones and kids running around popped in her head and the image was definitely appealing.

She sighed and scooped the last of the carrots into the pot.

Time would tell.

* * *

Torie tossed the covers off her legs in a huff. Sleep was not happening for her. Not tonight.

The four of them had stayed up late talking, catching up and hearing stories from Dane and Aimee about their trip. It was nice to laugh and get her mind off what was happening tomorrow. Even Keith's brow furrowed less. But he clung to her all evening, never leaving her side. And that was fine with her.

Now, alone with only her thoughts to keep her company, she fought to ignore the knot in her gut. Keith would go Lord knows where tomorrow, and she would head back to her world in San Diego. Face her past. Was she really ready?

She threw on boots over her yoga pants and grabbed her heavy coat. Moving stealthily through the house, she could hear Dane snoring down the hall. Good. He and Aimee were out cold. Finding her keys, she sneaked out to her truck, grateful she'd parked it away from the house. With the way Dane was snoring, there was no way he or Aimee would hear her.

What compelled her to go to the barn, she had no clue. In her restlessness, all she could think of was how at peace she was when riding Patsy. She longed to be near the horses.

She parked in the back. The barn wasn't far from the main house and she didn't want to chance waking Colt or Ellie.

Using the flashlight from her truck, she went through the back door and made her way through the workout area to the front of the barn where the stalls were. The smell of hay filled her nose as it crunched beneath her boots. Sensing her there, Patsy poked her head out of her stall. Torie walked over to her and rubbed her soft nose. The horse's warm breath puffed out into the cold air like clouds.

Torie took a deep breath. She would miss this place. Miss the peace that surrounded her here.

Patsy lifted her head, her ears pointing backwards. Torie sensed her tension and knew before she even turned someone was there.

"Well now, haven't we turned into quite the little cowgirl."

Her blood ran cold. In slow motion, she turned. Moonlight shone through one of the windows along the top of the barn, making out his silhouette in the dark. "Come on now, Victoria. Don't you have a hug for your old man?"

22

TORIE'S KNEES SHOOK beneath her. She widened her stance to support herself better. She might be afraid, but she'd be damned if she'd let her dad know it.

He took a step towards her into the moonlight. Able to see his face now, she didn't recoil the way she thought she would. It had been what...about fourteen years since she'd seen him. And time hadn't been his friend. Wrinkles covered his face, age and drinking had weathered him.

They were the same height now, an advantage for her but only in defending herself. Not in the fact that she was eye-to-eye with him. That meant she could see straight into the one thing that hadn't changed—the look that bore into her, told her she was worthless. The brown beady eyes filled with nothing but disgust.

Funny thing though, he didn't frighten her the way he did when she was a child. All the years with Gram, the time spent training to be a police officer—those years had changed her too. And Keith. Keith's love showed her what she was truly worth. Her value.

She searched the barn behind her dad and in her peripheral vision for anything she could use as a weapon. The workout part of the barn had some items that would work, but she'd have to get past him to do that.

"So, you went and made yourself a police officer. Isn't that ironic."

"How did you find me?"

He threw his head back and laughed. "Now that's a funny story. I started looking for Victoria Adler. Had to scratch my head over finding that she doesn't really much exist anymore." He took a step to his right, one hand in his jean pocket, the other scratching the back of his neck.

His movement allowed Torie to see into the workout area better, but she was still way too far away to grab anything worthwhile.

His eyes bore into her once again as he continued. "It took me a bit to actually swallow that my own daughter would change her name. Take her mama's maiden name. What? Mine wasn't good enough for you?"

"Nothing about you was ever good enough for me." How she found her voice she had no clue. But she was grateful. Courage began to bubble inside her, rising more and more with each breath.

He narrowed his eyes at her. "Is that so?"

"You still haven't said how you found me." Curiosity motivated her questions, as well as needing him to keep talking, stay distracted so she could think about her next move.

"That's right. The funny part of this story. That no-good excuse of a brother you have, believe it or not, actually stepped up for once."

What? Torie couldn't believe it. Her brother would never betray her like that.

"You see, that's the beauty of a druggie. They do, or say, just about anything if you give them cash for their next hit."

"He was doing better, trying to get clean."

"Trying and succeeding are two different things, little girl. And here's the funny part. The idiot actually has a damn Facebook page. Made it easier than I could've hoped to find him."

Crap. Seriously? The police department used social media all the time to find criminals, people dumb enough to air their laundry to the world thinking only "friends" would see it. She just never pegged her brother to be that dense.

Torie took two slow steps to her right. This caused her father to do the same, the two of them circling one another like two opponents before a wrestling match.

"So he gave you my name and phone number. That doesn't explain how you found me *here*."

"Ah, the beauty of the Internet once more. I googled the name Torie Walker," he said with a snarl. "Come to find a nice article about you helping to take down some big name drug dude. Had a nice picture of you and everything. It was nice of the story to say exactly where that bust went down. Since you weren't in San Diego"—he shrugged—"I took a shot in the dark you'd come here to hide. Great minds think alike now, don't they?"

Torie's blood curdled. She and her father were nothing alike. Never were. Never would be.

Another step or two and she'd be in a position to make a run for the workout room, possibly the back door. Either way, she'd be able to grab a barbell or anything she could whip around and toss at her father's head. The handled weight of a kettlebell would do it. "What do you want?"

"What do I want?" He chuckled, an evil twinge to it that echoed through the barn. "I want revenge, sweetheart." He took another step to the right but then one towards her. "You see, you took from me the only woman I have ever loved, or will ever love."

Now it was Torie's turn to laugh. "You never loved Mom. You never loved any of us. You controlled us."

His eyes narrowed and he clenched his fists. "Shut up! You've got no clue what you're talking about, little girl."

"Stop calling me that. I'm not a little girl anymore and I was *never* your little girl."

A shiver ran up and down her spine as he looked her over. She swallowed the urge to vomit. "Oh you were my little girl, but you're right, not anymore. Quite the beauty you turned out to be. Just like your mama. Too bad she's not here instead of you. But I'm about to change that."

The courage that had been brewing gushed through her system. "Give it your best shot."

The taunting had the desired effect. He lunged for her but she was ready. In a flash, she took off towards the back of the barn, her father losing his footing and slamming into the horse stall that was right behind where Torie had been standing. Thank God she was younger and faster.

She ran with the devil at her back, her father's footsteps now gaining on her. Knowing the layout of the barn better than him worked to her advantage. Heading for her weapon of choice, she grabbed the kettlebell and spun. It hit her dad in the torso, knocking him to his back with a thud.

The barn door creaked. She didn't have to look. She knew who was there.

Her father's moans echoed through the quiet barn. "What the...? Who the hell are you?" Her father spit, blood spewing across hay. He looked from the doorway to Torie. "You chose one hell of a huge rescuer, little girl."

"She's not your little girl. And I would imagine from your view down there, you can see she doesn't need me to rescue her. But you can be damn sure I've got her back."

Torie turned her head, the kettlebell still gripped in her hand. Keith took up the doorway, his legs spread apart and his arms crossed over his chest. Damn, if he wasn't the sexiest thing she'd ever seen.

He looked from her father to her. "You okay?"

She set down the kettlebell. "Never better."

Sirens blared in the distance, cutting through the quiet night.

"And that's *my* backup." Keith winked at her.

* * *

Keith sat on a hay bale with Torie and watched as the cops cuffed her dad and put him in a squad car. Based on him violating parole and coming after his daughter, the man would be behind bars again for quite some time. Nothing made Keith happier. Well, the woman sitting beside him sure did.

"You gave me a scare tonight, Dragonfly."

She smiled. Her eyes were tired but otherwise she was no worse for wear. Thank God. If that man had laid one hand on her, God help him. Jail was a welcome choice over what Keith would've done to him.

"I have to admit I was a bit scared myself."

"But you faced him. Took him down, even. And with a kettle bell. That's a first, I think."

Her laugh warmed his insides. "Believe me, I definitely wished I'd had my gun with me."

"Why didn't you?"

She shook her head. "I was just coming to the barn to say good-bye to Patsy. I never thought I needed to be armed."

"Then you need to think different. I'm always armed."

Her eyes moved up and down his body, searching for where said weapons could be. Oh, she could search for them all she wanted. That was fine by him. He leaned over and kissed her.

"What was that for?"

"I just couldn't help myself."

"You can help yourself anytime you want." She kissed him back then laid her head on his shoulder. "How'd you know where I was?"

"Aimee. She heard you leave in your truck and called me. Had a bad feeling."

"I'd like to say I'm sorry I woke you guys, but I'm not."

"I was awake. I'm always restless before I leave. And Bones was twitchy. I had a bad feeling too. Dane found a rundown car outside our property line so he called a friend at the police department. Said he thought someone might be on our property. Turns out he was right."

Torie tucked her arm under his and took his hand. "I'm so sorry, Keith. I'm sorry I brought this on you and your family. It's so peaceful here. I didn't mean to ruin that."

"You didn't ruin anything, Torie. We protect our own in the Scott family. And I'm just relieved to know your dad is behind bars again. I can leave without that worry."

She lifted her head and looked at him. Her hazel eyes glimmered with tears but none fell. "I want you to leave without worrying. You need to stay focused over there, not be distracted with anything going on here."

He nodded. "I'll be thinking about you though, that's for sure."

"And I you." She took his face in her hands and kissed him. A tender, slow kiss that might have lasted hours, he couldn't tell. Didn't want to. It was a moment he would take with him, relive over and over while he was gone.

When she pulled back, she looked him in the eye. "You do your job and come home to me, you understand? I'll be fine. I'll be here praying you home."

No sweeter words had been said to him in his lifetime. No woman had ever meant more. His life, all he cared about and loved he wrapped up in his arms and held until the sun rose on the horizon.

* * *

Six Months Later

Rae hadn't been lying when she said it was tough. Being away from Keith was hard for Torie, but the worst part was not knowing where he was or what he was doing. If he was alive or not. In some ways no news was good news. In some ways, it wasn't.

She waited for calls from him, many times their conversations benign and simple. He couldn't give away any information, so the calls were mainly validation that he was alive.

She prayed more in those times than any other in her life. And she'd kept his coat, the one he'd given her the first night he kissed her cheek. Some nights she'd wrap herself up in that just to be closer to him, breathe in his scent that clung to the fabric, and pray him home.

Torie waited behind the gate with the other family members. A toddler squatted next to his mother, a small American flag in his chubby little grasp. The mother held a small infant wrapped in a pink blanket. Some held signs welcoming their loved ones home. Joy was in the air, almost tangible.

Keith had gone on two missions in the past six months. Each lasting about eight weeks. Each time being the longest eight weeks of Torie's life. Even with the distance though, she was closer to Keith than anyone in her life. She'd never been in a relationship where the physical aspect wasn't the most important. Of course, the attraction between them was there, but their connection came from conversation, friendship, sharing goals and future dreams.

When he was home, she'd spent as much time at the 4S Ranch as she could or he came to San Diego, but more and more, visions of marriage and family danced in her head. They'd talked about her moving to Tahoe, living closer. And she'd even interviewed with the police department there.

Her girly side had to admit, she dreamed of a winter wedding. One not unlike the infamous Scott Christmas parties. She in a mermaid style white dress and a fur wrap around her shoulders, and Keith in his Marine Corps dress uniform. Man, that uniform was beautiful, even more so when her man was in it. Dancing out under the stars, their perfect winter wonderland.

A large plane pulled up and stopped not far from where she and the others stood. A stairway was pulled up to it and soliders emerged. One by one, they descended the steps, each branching off to hug loved ones. Amidst cheers and shouts of "Daddy!" Torie spotted him. He reached the tarmac and headed towards her. Not one to have ever thought camouflage attractive, she now found it downright sexy. Right up there with his jeans and cowboy boots.

His big dimpled grin and ice-blue eyes drew her in like a tractor beam. He dropped his gear and opened his arms wide. Who was she to disappoint the man? She flew into his embrace and wrapped herself around him, the rest of the world floating away.

"Hey Dragonfly." His breath was warm against her neck.

"Welcome home, Captain."

"I've got a question for you and I can't wait to ask anymore."

She pulled back and held his face in her hands.

"Ask away."

His blue eyes twinkled, causing her tummy to flip. "Marry me?"

Joy bubbled up inside her, her smile wide. "Oh yes, definitely."

He kissed her. A kiss full of passion and a promise to make her dreams come true.

The End

ACKNOWLEDGMENTS

So much goes on behind the scenes to create a book. Yes, the writing is key, but there is so much more beyond that. People who work hard, encourage, and make the journey possible from idea to actual book form.

Thank you, Crystal Posey, for being my literal right hand. For gorgeous book covers, formatting, marketing, and basically keeping me on track, sane, and making it fun to get up each day and do this writing gig. Your constant encouragement means the world to me. You are truly the best.

Thank you, Laura Shin. Editing is my least favorite part of this process and you honestly make it fun for me (which is saying a lot). I greatly appreciate your flexibility with my schedule and how you make the process seamless and enjoyable.

The ECC Quilting group. Thank you for welcoming me into the fold when I came to you with a simple desire to learn how to quilt yet had never sewn before in my life and didn't own a sewing machine. Your kindness, your laughter, your friendship has become a most cherished community to me, and I adore you all.

My family. Thank you for listening as I verbally processed characters and story. Thank you for making research fun. Thank you for your patience with me during the writing process when I hole up for hours in my office and for all the years you have been my biggest cheerleaders. I love you bunches.

ABOUT THE AUTHOR

Writing stories since she was a young girl, Lara's dream of being a novelist became a reality with her Men of Honor series. An avid reader, she worked as a book reviewer for 18 years with various organizations. She has a BA in Journalism and a Masters of Divinity in Chaplaincy. Lara loves tea, baseball and living in Idaho with her husband and Great Dane. You can find Lara online at www.laramvanhulzen.com

ALSO BY LARA

The Endicotts of Silver Bay Series
Love at Meg's Diner, Book One
Christmas Cakes and Kisses, Book Two
Until I Met You, Book Three
An Angel for Christmas, Book Four

The Silver Bay Series
Return to Silver Bay, Book One
Loving Kate, Book Two
Saving Drew, Book Three
Hannah's Hope, A Novella

The Marietta St. Claire Series
A Recipe for Romance, Book One
Winning His Heart, Book Two
His Christmas Bride, Book Three
Finding Her Montana Cowboy, Book Four

The Men of Honor Series
Remember Me, Book One
Get to Me, Book Two
Rescue Me, Book Three

Single Titles
I Grew Up Dancing: Celebrating the Joy of Knowing Jesus
(daily devotional)
Guarding Paragon (young adult fiction)

Made in the USA
Monee, IL
25 August 2025